LEEDS LIBRARY AND INFORMATION SERVICE

Please return/renew thi
Overdue charges may a

22-01-2020

2 2 APR 2025

AF

LD 3445675 9

The author's Edixa Reflex 35MM camera which features in the text and which, if it could speak, might tell such a story

ON ENCOUNTERING
ANGELS AND SIRENS

By Basil John

Cover Illustration: 'La mandra' by Ramon Casas
Carbo (1866-1932)

Photograph of 'Wendy' on page 156
© 2017 John Ridyard

This book is based on true events.

The majority of the text was first published 2011
under the title: SHARING: An Imperfect
Recollection
This edition is Copyright © 2017 John Ridyard

All rights are reserved.

Contents

PROLOGUE
Stranded in the Night
London King's Cross
The River
An Angel
Sukie
Walking alone in the Fog
Dancers
Uncle Pierre
Detectives and Foxes
The Mansions
Home at Last
Jules's Madonna in Red
On Trial
A dream of Sukie
Jules's Bedfellow
Wendy's Accident
Waking into a Dream
Imaginings
A Distraction
Breakfast
Uncle Pierre and Men with Guns
Imagined Futures
A Bunch of Flowers
Reality returns
At Garelochhead Station
End Notes

PROLOGUE

'But I would love to live in a big City ... like Edinburgh or London ... it's *all* my mum's fault I don't ... when she was my age she lived in swinging nineteen-sixties London ... had a rich boyfriend too ... just how lucky was that? ... But she had to play the hero ... didn't she ... so my sister and me ... we must be hidden away, behind her skirts, in the back of beyond...'

The voice is young with a slight hint of a London accent, and, after she'd paused a moment or two to catch her breath and to cast a cursory glance out of the carriage window at the slowly changing wild scenery,

'... but honest ... Mr Paul ...when all you get to see every day, is mountains and stuff ... it's dead boring; The only good thing is that we ... my big sister and me, get to shoot our mum's rifle ... It has a telescope sight and everything ... and we get to carry our own little automatics ... But that has to be a huge secret ... the pistols bit ... so what's so cool about that?'
The girl speaks other words too: - 'protection', murder', 'rape', 'corruption' and phrases: - 'you know ... men like the Cray brothers and those Richardson's,' which, when combined with '...

had to hide away in the back of beyond ...' shake Jules out of his half –sleep to focus his mind as surely as if her words were the ringing of an alarm clock … a girl's words out of place and out of time… to waken his past.

Today is August bank holiday 1994 and Jules is riding on a long train of careworn carriages, pulled by an equally careworn diesel locomotive; it is meandering unhurriedly through highland scenery towards Glasgow and apart from himself, Paul, his travelling companion, the young woman, and their combined luggage – a battered old suitcase and the several soft bags which fill the nearby seating – the carriage is empty. The three are returning from a sailing holiday and Jules is in that peculiar state, between wakefulness and sleep, a situation which has allowed Paul an opportunity to monopolise the girl, who was a member of the tall ships.

      Their exchanges are reminiscences of sailing the Brigantine; its passengers and its crew; the sturdy wooden ship, its many ports of call and talk of the many interesting people they had met during their little ships stuttering voyage from Rouen to Oban.

      But now under the Svengali like influence of the old man, the focus of their quiet conversation has turned seamlessly to the girl; her future; her ambitions and her background.

      Paul is deeply interested in people and, on discovering that her name is Holly and today is her birthday, he tells her it is his too, but unlike hers, it is not his twenty-first.

Jules is sitting opposite, admiring while 'sleeping', the technique of his friend – imagining the old man's fine education and easy manner, combined with his charming smile and soft voice, would make him an excellent spy – an intelligence gatherer extraordinaire – and one able to seduce any pretty woman who might take his fancy. [1]

And he has not lost his touch, the girl, delighted by the old man's gentle attentiveness, or sensed that this harmless indulgence – this flirting – might be his last, is revealing a little of her and her mother's history.

A history which now bombards Jules's mind with a kaleidoscope of images; some so enchanting, as they flash through his mind, he wonders why they were ever suppressed … and so transient now… and why is it he cannot hold them still long enough to savour there beauty.

But there are others there too, some which might explain the loss; images not so beautiful … many formed during a single day ... the fourth of November nineteen sixty three.

A day he must re-live, which began on a train.

Stranded in the Night

Jules is sitting alone on a train, but this train is not one meandering through a sunlit picturesque Scottish glen… this train is standing silent and still in the dead of night; a mail-train which, for reasons unknown to him, has moved only a few hundred yards during the last two hours – and one of those dragging hours had belonged to the previous day.

When it first came to this grinding stop he'd put down his book 'The Hidden Persuaders' [2] to discover the carriage was, or at least seemed to be, perched on a low embankment surrounded by a magical moonlit nocturne complete with iridescent clouds reflected in a broad shallow lake, or flooded fields.

It was quite enchanting, but before he could properly take in its beauty a luminous mist, which had at first only softened the far distance, claimed the middle ground to cloak everything there. And almost before that scene could be remembered, the last of the increasingly fragile moonlight was lost to leave pitch darkness. All there is to see, beyond the greasy finger marks left by countless others, is swirls of fog clawing at the outside , and as if a ghost, his own face staring back at him.

The haunted look fitted his mood; reminded him of recent events; some he had no real wish to recall, so he pulled down the blind and returned to his book 'Galbraith's The hidden persuaders' But he was weary of it and put it aside in favour of a crumpled second or third hand newspaper whose front page strap headline read – 'Thousand a Year coppers Corrupt' – and further down the same page – 'Cuban rockets can reach Washington – Confirmed' World news ... if news it was.

'So what' came into his mind?

And as if the carriage agreed with his sentiment, the light emanating from the single incandescent bulb set in the roof of the compartment, faded from nicotine yellow – to dull orange – to feeble red – to blackness.

There are no distractions to prevent sleep now; no passing scenery; no soothing noises from the train, not even the gentle repetitive puffing of air-brakes from the distant locomotive, so now his mind is filling with 'stuff'; New Stuff collected during the last few days; stuff begging to be put into order and into some kind of focus.

He'd known it had been a crazy dream; a foolish ideal. After all who in the world gets to marry their first lover; especially when her father has forbidden any thought of it? But regardless of this he and his Sukie had made their plan, believing that the power of their love could overcome everything.

All Jules must do is complete his post diploma year in London; get a good and well paid job... no problem ... a nice house; build up a healthy bank balance etc. and her Father would change his mind in an instant.

OK it might take the odd year or so, but 'so what' that would be no problem. The only difficult thing, for them both, would be them being apart and deprived of the opportunity to make their special 'love' quite so often; And for Jules, the slight chance 'his' Sukie's heart might be stolen from him.

He knows that many might try, because when she was at Art School her beauty had been hidden away from all but him; hidden away beneath the universal 'uniform' of floppy sweater, jeans and donkey jacket. But that veil had gone for ever now; banished by a dead white and shape-revealing ribbed sweater; charcoal grey box pleat mini skirt; a shiny black raincoat with matching patent shoulder-bag and heeled shoes – a combination which showed her to be as elegant and as beautiful as any film star – a fact proved to Jules when he'd seen her … just a few days ago … crossing the busy streets towards her place of work. She had taken his eye and that of everyone else, including those of the bus and taxi-drivers.

It had been the weekend before Jules had left for London and his love, having just turned seventeen, had stopped the rush hour traffic.

To leave the art school had not been her choice, she had loved it from the first moment of the very first day, and she'd wished to continue to study at another college, but her father had put a stop to 'all that nonsense' and insisted she 'got a proper job'; It was a decision which came, out of the blue.

They, Sukie and her father, had been looking through her portfolio together; a viewing, she believed, born of genuine interest and a mere preliminary to his blessing being freely given. And in support of this impression her father had muttered faint praise as each page was turned (he is of a generation to which giving or receiving any other level of praise was unthinkable) and all had been well until they came to her life drawings – those made from the female nude – where he became suddenly and alarmingly incensed, condemning every single one as '... a pile of rubbish only fit for the fire ...' and the tutors responsible '... corrupting and incompetent'.

And in the next moment the whole body of work was polluted with that same 'infection' and with a fire made outside in the garden, Sukie – filled with fear, was made to place each sheet in the flames herself; and, when every single artwork on paper had been reduced to a memory, her prints on fabric followed; and then her note books, until all evidence of the last two years – those six-hundred wonderful days of pure joy – was lost in flames. All that remained was her memory of them and of Jules – she would always have Jules – But then the pearl ring which they'd chosen together as an outward declaration of her virginity – in the face of all temptation – was sent for, and cast into the fire with a demand that she must never see him ever again; a cruel sentence, commuted after

pleadings by her compassionate but equally terrified mother, to a year apart. [3]
Sukie had submitted to her father's demand, having no choice, but Jules when confronted with the idea, had not. Instead he'd quietly let her father rant on at him, declaring how he and his dear wife had not brought Sukie into this world for her to be wasted on some feckless art student.

Jules had listened politely, answering silently

'Sir', (the man was after all his senior and the father of the girl he wished to marry) *'I know your daughter is precious. ... Tell me about it. She is precious to me too ... You know, but no you wouldn't, in another time she could have posed for Waterhouse's 'Sirens'; Even Ruskin would have been hard pressed to find a fault (if he overlooked her feet being a little long and her knees not quite parallel), but what you can't know is this ... she is so much more than just a beautiful young woman... She is filled with magic.*

I suspected it after our very first kiss; and then some time after ... You see, from that kiss we progressed to share much more ... and afterwards when I looked into her eyes ... past the surface of her rainbow filled eyes ... I discovered another world ... There is a heaven in there ... all of perfect creation, with all the wonder of it; colourful spinning spiral galaxies, planets ... the lot. And when I look into her eyes I can dive through all that wonder ... to 'her' earth ... her inner world ... where every corner is filled with peace and love ... sun-lit meadows and clear sparkling streams ... a whole blinking beautiful world ... Her inner world ... full to overflowing with peace and beauty.

To you, my dear sir, Sukie might seem a wilful, sometimes disobedient teenager, but to her friends who have sensed her inner beauty, she is pure sunshine. And to me she is even more ... an Angel a Supernatural and my compelling desire is to be with her all the time ... and for us to travel to her heaven and be there together just as often as we can'. And in his conclusion he might have said,

'And you (SIR) dare to tell me ... ask me ... to stay away from her ... you may as well tell me to stop the world turning ... NO CHANCE'.

But he can't tell anyone of these adventures. He hadn't even dared tell Sukie, fearing she had not felt the same and might think him to be 'strange' or 'weird'.

So all he can say to her father is,

'I'm sorry, but I care too much for Sukie to do what you ask. She is so special to me it would only be an empty promise'.

There is a jolt and the train begins to move accompanied by a momentary squeal of metal against metal, and to Jules's delight the dynamo beneath his feet begins to turn – he can feel the slight vibration – and the light bulb glows a dismal red, but in a few moments the train is still again and the silence and blackness returns allowing him to recall and re-live the last few days.

It had been half-term, a break from study filled with hope of good news about his father's health and a joyous reunion with Sukie, but as the days had passed; one horror had stacked upon the last, until he'd begun to believe it might have been better for him to have stayed in London.

But then he wouldn't have known his father's eyesight had failed completely – but not his wonderful insight – or that Sukie's night school teacher had asked for a goodnight kiss and, after being foolishly granted it, expected more.

'My *lovely; lonely abandoned Sukie ... what were you thinking of ?'*

And their art student go-between – Janette:-

Had she fallen for Sukie and that was why she'd failed to pass on Jules's love-letters? ... Such a good looking girl too ... I wonder if they were ever alone together ... and they had kissed ... or if she and Sukie had ever made love.

And the Cafe proprietor who Jules had reluctantly charged with keeping a watchful eye on Sukie – reluctantly, because he suspected he 'liked her' far too much; supplied cannabis to the local students; and when it wasn't on his person, kept a .38 Webley and \Scott revolver behind the cafe counter – had he, Stanton, even though he'd been expressly forbidden, taken advantage of Sukie's loneliness and seriously over stepped his remit?

But, in case any of these fears might be true, last Saturday evening when Sukie was on her way home from work, he'd contrived to be at her bus stop. At first behind her and out of view in the milling crowd of commuters, and then, as her bus arrived, standing next to his her as she stepped on-board and a few moments later, sitting next to her on the upper deck. All so he might re-declare his love for her.

It had, he believed, been a last chance, and there, in this confined but public space he had whispered that he would always love her … no matter what.

But now he has no recollection of his precise words only that some close-bye passengers had clapped their appreciation as he disembarked … one or two insisting on shaking his hand and risking him missing his stop.

And just yesterday, after the rain had stopped and the sun was making the winters day unusually warm, he'd had the best conversation he'd ever had with his 'Dad' in which they'd talked of nature, dancing, electricity and the magic of girls – all of whom, according to the older and blinded man, must have their secrets … It was, he confided, part of their mystery … and according to him, 'why we love them'.

It had been a gentle conversation, full of understanding, which quietened the inner screaming, which 'went' with unwelcome imaginings of Sukie in the arms of Stanton – Screaming which, according to his father, had, during the previous night, escaped the confines of his son's head to disturb the otherwise tranquil small hours – Sounds which Jules had no recollection of making, but might explain why he'd woken that morning to find his pillow cold and damp.

He had apologised with all his heart, knowing his parents had troubles enough.

His recollections stop. To his delight the mail train is moving and, to Jules's relief, the single light bulb recessed into the discoloured roof of the compartment responds and remains bright – the dynamo is spinning – humming its own tuneless tune -- at last, he, the Royal Mail and the parcel post are on their way to the terminus at Kings Cross where all will disperse – the post to who knows where – while Jules hails a taxi to take him across the City to Waterloo station, from where he plans to walk the mile or so to the Mansions. There to find his bed and welcome sleep.

London

The train could have been motionless at Kings Cross station for some little time before Jules woke to realise his journey was over. And the station was deserted; even the branch of W.H. Smith was sleeping, together with its stock of colourful magazines, behind its shabby roller shutter. There is a stock of this morning papers stacked outside in uneven towers, each tied with coarse string and others marked for return and pulping.

The only movements, an electric tractor snaking, its unruly train of caged trucks filled with parcels through an archway to Jules's left, and in front, as he hesitated beside the great heat and deafening thunder of the resting locomotive, a janitor sweeping idly at, what seemed to Jules, a pile of imagined litter.

He glanced around and as there was no one in sight to challenge him, he stuffed his ticket back in his overcoat pocket and, passing the gated and locked entrance to the Underground; he left the station and the temporary warmth of the locomotive and made his way through the brick archway which led to the cold outside world and the taxi-rank.

There was just one old style London Taxicab standing there… A god-send … and it was warmish inside.

The only problem being, when Jules gave his destination, the driver would not go south of the River. However he would be delighted to go half way across any bridge of Jules's choosing, explaining …'It's more than my life's worth and that of mi' wife and kids if I go any further … last time cost me four new tyres …That's what you get down 'ere for picking up the wrong fare and asking for it.'

'No problem …' said Jules,'… you can drop me on Waterloo Bridge … I can easily walk the rest'.

The River

It is four in the morning and a mist, iridescent in the moonlight, has formed over the Thames, drawn up by the freezing air, to leave only the defused glow from the Dolphin Lamps to indicate its course. And, as Jules walks south, that freezing vapour grows and claws its way over the parapet to swirl around his feet.

Jules has seen this bridge in paintings by Whistler and Monet and recollects one which included, for effect, a steam vessel; and, as if to compliment that idea, when he is a little over half way across, a tug slides out of nowhere to pass beneath him, its exhaust adding swirling shapes and faintly sulphurous smoke to the already softly coloured atmosphere.

It makes him stop to stand on the downstream side, to enjoy, as the steam disperses, a fleeting glimpse of it; and to hear, if he can, over the rushing sound of so much displaced water, the breathing of its engine. But he can't – it is as noiseless as a ghost – but the fruit of its gallant work is clear enough, for under the vessels stern the dark unwilling river is transformed into swirling dirty foam by its huge propeller pushing hard against the last of an incoming tide.

Close behind are two huge steel swim-headed barges, groaning as if in protest at the heavy chains and cables which bind them to their master and to each other. They are brim full of refuse – a sight which at any another time would be ugly – but now, decorated by sparkling haw frost and illuminated by moonlight, they look like a pair of gigantic fruit pies sprinkled with sugar.

And when the last one has passed into the night and the water has settled back into a dark stillness, he cannot help but recall yesterday and his last meeting with his father, which had also been their very first true 'heart to heart'; one Jules had known, in his own heart, would also be their last. The older blinded man might have felt the same and, after Jules had expressed his heartache at seeing his love with another man, he'd said

'... but Jules ... you should know a woman's heart is like a broad and deep river ... full of secrets never to be told ... it is part of their mystery ... it is why we love them ...' words which had made Jules wonder, for a moment, what secret could possibly sleep inside his mother's heart, before promising himself and his father that whatever else he might achieve in life – first in his mind would be to adore and protect his love – his Sukie.

An Angel

A woman's voice; a bright cultured and gentle sound cuts the darkness

'Would you like a nice, hot, mug of tea?'

Its pleasant abruptness wakes him from his day-dreaming and he turns to see what he imagines at first to be an Angel because its lower half is lost in the swirl of fog left behind by the tug. But it isn't; it is a woman in her middle years; smart; well-spoken and here, in the dead of night, completely out of place; and with her right hand – no, both of her hands and her arms extended towards him as if their gentle owner was offering not what she had suggested, but salvation or hope; a suggestion, so strong it is all he can do to top himself blurting out

'I wasn't going to jump ... I hadn't even thought of it ... Honest ... You wouldn't believe the amazing future I have ahead of me.'

But before he could compose a less panic stricken reply the 'Angel' says

' ... We have a kitchen nearby ... outside Waterloo Station ... it's only a very few steps way ... please come'.

Her arms are still outstretched as if inviting an embrace, and Jules answers

'Yes thank you' because there is that 'something' about the lady which prevents him refusing, or telling her his London home and bed are only a few hundred yards away – it would, he feared, have seemed ungrateful or ill-mannered; especially as it must have been obvious to her that, close to home or not, he was shivering and his overnight case was tied to his left wrist.

The 'Kitchen' is a relic of the last war; a field kitchen mounted on an Austin lorry chassis. It is painted the colour of sand and has probably seen service in the searing heat of North Africa, but is now in the service of the W. V. S., providing a little comfort for some of London's homeless, some of whom are sitting close-by on the pavement, or stuffing newspaper inside their clothing; an action Jules has never seen before and he pretends not to notice as he passes to collect his 'tea' which, when he takes a sip, is unlike any he has tasted before, not even when dispensed from similar vehicles at air displays. The plus side is it warms him from the inside; the downside is an instant blister on his upper lip.

One of the men 'stuffing' is a man wearing a once very smart, but now polished pin-striped suit, who is guarding a shabby briefcase; and when Jules sits down next to him the man offers an answer to Jules's un-asked question

' ... Evening Standard.... the others assure me it is by far the best ... I used The Times to begin with ... the financial pages ... so I might find my failing stocks had recovered, but they didn't and it cut me to ribbons in more ways than one. There's plenty here ... The dear sweet lady, who brought you over, persuaded the van driver to leave them for us ... Bloody nice of her ... and him don't you think? Would you like some?'

Jules refuses politely and then, putting his 'tea' down, asks the man if he might let the 'dear sweet lady', who is out of his view, know that when she returns to discover he has gone, he has left to sleep in a warm and comfortable bed and is not lost to her caring and in the river.

Jules turns then and has begun to walk south towards the entry to Low Marsh when he remembers his manners and calls back to the man,

'Good luck to you ... and please tell the dear lady she is really sweet ... an Angel ... and give her my thanks for everything ... including the 'tea'.

In Low Marsh the sound of every step echoes in the silence, the repeated sound sometimes tricking him into imagining he is being followed, but he is alone, with only his most private thoughts for company and a persistent piece of litter, driven by an invisible wind, to keep him company.

It is sometimes in front of him and seeming to guide the way, but more often floating at his side, and when close he can see tidy handwriting which gives Jules the idea that it might be a lost love-letter. So out of curiosity, he tries to capture it, but after a few failed attempts he is convinced that the green-blue writing, which is fast dissolving into the paper, has no desire to be read, so he imagines another letter – one intended for him – one from Sukie, which, if he was to receive it, he might wish to read over and over again.

What he will never know is that it is already written; composed only a few hours ago when his love had dared recall being a carefree art student and Jules's willing muse.

Sukie

Her art school – was a wondrous place which overlooked a huge park and enjoyed the external appearance of a French château or a Fairy-tale Castle. It even had a small turret which jutted out from the first floor with a tiny widow from which a love-lorn princess might let down a long plait of her golden hair for a handsome lover to climb.

And inside it was even more incredible – a labyrinth of corridors and staircases connecting innumerable rooms, all of different shapes and sizes; some lofty and proportioned in Regency style with ornate plaster ceilings, bay windows and hinged internal shutters; others, little more than large cupboards; tiny, low, and secretive.

Most of the larger rooms have no tables, or desks, or chairs, instead they are littered with tall and heavy wooden easels, with sticking out legs for the unwary to trip over; stepped wooden platforms and strange low benches. And everywhere, tucked away in corners to surprise the unwary, are plaster casts taken from Roman or Greek classical sculpture. Anyone could tell that they were old because they were chipped and had some bits missing.

And as if these appearances were not enough – and despite the school lying empty for the summer holiday – there was the smell; a heady cocktail of turpentine, white spirit and oil paint which reminded Sukie of when her father was painting doors and woodwork at home, but this was much heavier.

As for her fellow students – it was easy to identify the painters because their working clothes were splattered with paint of every colour imaginable, and had a peculiar old clothes smell about them.

And the Etchers and Lithographers – their clothes had a less familiar smell; less aromatic, but equally heady, with a hint of sulphur. They had ragged holes in them too, burned by splashes of acid; and had splodges of ink -- mostly black – which let everyone know what they were.

This group which included Jules, worked in a string of tiny sky lighted rooms which had once been hay lofts set over stables – stables that now served as pottery studios – which bounded one side of a central area which had once been a cobbled turning space for horse drawn carriages, but was now a massive glass roofed hall dedicated to the making of sculpture in metal, clay or plaster. It had its own smell too; a background musty smell of damp plaster – slightly scented – on occasion swamped by the smell of burning and clouds of acrid smoke accompanied by a cacophony of excited voices.

There were two ways into the print rooms; one through a low and narrow doorway cut through a thick wall part-way down a first floor corridor and another at the top of a steep and narrow stairway. The first had steps too, so everyone who entered had to duck their head while avoiding curtains of damp paper hung with pegs from strings like washing on lines. There were thick fumes too, from acid burning into metal and the heady smell of shellac, ink and solvents which created a powerful barrier to deter all but those with a powerful reason to enter, and were wearing suitable clothes – a place in which William Hogarth re-incarnated would have felt at his ease, with no machine, chemical or other part of the processes of printmaking changed since his time.

This is where Jules worked most afternoons, grinding a lithographic stone clean of a redundant image, 'burning' an etching plate or toiling at one of the hand cranked presses. These rooms were dangerous places and forbidden territory for all but printmakers (A notice to this effect, made using huge wooden type, was one of the very few, if not the only, health and safety rule in the entire school).

Sue soon discovered that the strange benches in the larger rooms were called 'donkeys', because of there vague resemblance to that animal, when used as low sit-upon easels. The donkey's 'neck' forming an angled support for a drawing board and its back a seat for the artist with a storage well for drawing materials – pencils, board clips, rubbers, chalks and stuff.

It was an arrangement which made the user work at arm's length; which was supposed to be a good thing, as it prevented 'precious' work and provided the artist with a continuous distant over-view of their efforts; so the teachers said.

The first time Sue used one she'd discovered that mounting the beast was impossible to do with any dignity, especially if caught out wearing a dress or skirt, and on her first time she was wearing a skirt.

She had watched the others around her – one of whom had stood astride the bench, hitched up her voluminous skirt, and, holding it around her as though it was a huge nappy, sat down quickly shooting her legs out in front. But it proved not a good idea, as the girl was left holding her skirt in the air to prevent it falling into the well and becoming covered with chalk. They'd each looked at each other and burst into quiet laughter, giggling really. Sue – Sue was the other girls name too – had proved that her nappy technique was not a good idea and they became immediate friends.

Then it dawned on them – that this method might just work – all they had to do was gather their skirts behind them; so together they hitched up, reached under themselves and, from the back this time, pulled their skirts through and sat down using them as cushions. It worked perfectly – there was no difficulty in getting to the well now, and together they placed their drawing boards against the neck of their donkeys, and found pencils, chalk and paper.

Both had exposed an awful lot of their legs, as had most of the other girls and Sukie was a little self-conscious of hers – believing them thin and un-shapely when compared with most of the others she could see around her (her friend Sue's were quite heavy) – but it was short lived and faded away when the life model appeared from behind a folding screen.

At first she was hidden behind a dressing gown so large it could have folded around her several times – It had a lovely Chinese dragon design on it – And then, after a few moments, during which he said something to her, the teacher took it from her. It was all very theatrical and the room, which had been buzzing with so many whispered conversations, fell suddenly and totally silent.

She was facing the class, as still as still; her body as well-proportioned as any of the plaster statues which stood in a corner of the room, and just as naked. But unlike the statues she was alive and with no bits missing, a fully formed young woman in her early or mid-twenties – blonde and, if she had been wearing make-up – as beautiful as a fashion model. And when Sukie had looked around the young men in her year were looking at her as if they were petrified; all as still as stones.

It was then that Sukie looked at herself; at her legs, which looked even skinnier than ever against the bulk of the donkey; and at her knees, which she knew had a tendency to look at each other, and back to the model. Her legs are so straight and shapely; and her bust is nice too with pretty pink rosettes around quite big sticky-out nipples. And they're both equal in shape and size – unlike her own – but no one else would know, thanks to the folded tissues – And further down, under her tummy where the model has a dark triangle, she hasn't.

But she's not at all envious of that, and while she'd mused to herself the room around her had filled with sounds which would soon become familiar; the rustling of paper; the soft scraping of charcoal, chalk or pencil passing over paper; the sound of distant or whispered, but still overheard, encouragement from the tutor and the occasional sighs of exasperation as members of the 'virgin' group made tentative marks towards making their first ever life drawings.

There were Life studies, by more competent students pinned up around the studio and Sukie had looked at them for inspiration; some were in pencil, others drawn in charcoal or red crayon. And all the drawings of female models show them to be standing or lying down completely naked, and some had been drawn in awfully revealing poses and in intimate detail. And looking at them it made her think of those older men students who prowled the school wearing deep and serious expressions over old clothes, (both splattered with paint) – men who looked through her and other girls as they passed in the corridors – and she imagined that a normal girl, or any girl with her clothes on, might be invisible to them.

And then she noticed the drawings of a nude man and thanked goodness the man who had posed had a cover over his 'thing'.

And it was with these thoughts pushed aside that she'd begun her own first and very tentative life drawing.

She wasn't entirely sure she wanted to be noticed, not by some of the men anyway, because she could sense a terrible power raging inside them; like an invisible burning.

She knew this because if they caught her looking at them, their eyes would burn back – not speaking, but growling like some wild animal – saying 'speak to me if you dare.' It was terrifying, but also inexplicably attractive and she would close her eyes to hide the evidence. But she would always look again; and again; unable to stop herself.

One student; a tall man always in an old grey suit, whose eyes burned like those of a wolf, was so intense he terrified everyone including all but a few of the male students. But there were others who would return her shy glances and smile back; men who were not a lot older than her, who were interesting to look at and to have short conversations with. And then there was Jules, especially later after they'd kissed at the dance and been alone together and 'sharing'.

Everyone had dressed in his or her own way in the schools workshop environment – there was no uniformity – only the school scarf worn in the street. Some girls, when they knew they would be using the donkeys, would wear shrink to fit jeans or ski pants under a short dress or a very long sweater they'd knitted for themselves using needles made from wooden dowelling and yarn the gauge of thick string.

The men students and tutors alike just pulled on their oldest grey trousers or old Levi's, knowing that even if they tried to keep them clean, they would soon be plastered with paint, ink or clay; or covered with acid burns; or just worn through. The degree of distress was a sort of badge; an indication that the wearer belonged to an exclusive community and that he or she had won a place within it.

Those students who wished to be welcome in the town's café's and bars had an apron of some sort, to protect their more conventional wear, or had such clothes in their lockers.

Sukie had one – a real artist's smock – given to her as a fifteenth birthday present by her much older brother who lived away in London. It had been posted together with congratulations for gaining a place at Art school, but the prized garment had not remained pristine for long, as it soon gained a splash or two of paint and then 'mysteriously' two words appeared, probably written by the bearded tutor with the piercing blue-eyes, using his favourite brush – a long handled filbert – they read 'Sukie Sunshine' [5]

And now, so little time after, that smock is the only tangible reminder she has of those happy days and those gentle friends – all of whom she thought she'd lost for ever – until the closest of them had re-appeared, as if from nowhere, to declare he loved her and to promise he would always be true and come back to her – for her – whatever.

It had been the end of the summer when Jules had first made this promise, but so much had happened since then – between her and her father and between her father and Jules – including Sukie being told, unequivocally, she had seen the very last of the feckless Jules. But now, having seen him again, she'd dared to believe they might be together once more and with this dream sustaining her she'd laid tummy-down on her bed; propped herself on her elbows; opened a small pad of blue laid paper and begun to write. [6]

Walking alone in the Fog

Low March is a little forbidding – dank with condensing mist – and dark with only a very occasional street light to reveal walls punctuated by unlit windows and at ground level dark doorways and the ends of alleys which might lead to who-knows-where – brick caves with arched roofs and graphiti, which, when twilight fell on yesterday were pitches for working girls, or hide-outs for even younger pick-pockets.

But Jules feels safe enough – the feral children will be long-since tucked up in their beds, but perhaps still awake thinking how they might 'duck' school today – And the working girls, some of whom he has seen and believes to be far too young; or too pretty for such work, or almost too old, will be, after a cleansing bathe, in their beds too – enfolded in the arms of a caring comrade or enjoying welcome solitude. But still, as he steps from street light to street light, he cannot help but look into each doorway – not for want, or wish for 'comfort' – but in case there is someone huddled there, who, if he was brave enough to speak to them, he might help survive this bitter cold night by adding still more layers of newsprint to the endless mugs of scalding tea – both by courtesy of the posh lady with the sparkling eyes.

Jules knows this street and its shops – he and his flat mates had discovered it when furnishing their maisonette with this and that – it had proved a great place for bargains and on Saturdays when the street market filled every possible space and had provided everything they might wish for. [7] And the shop and stall keepers had quickly become friends – mostly through shared laughter when they'd tried, and failed, to understand each other's language.

The three still used these shops every Saturday morning to buy in provisions for the week ahead, while their shirts and bed linen were lodged at the Launderette and overseen by a group of gossipy women – It was now a long-standing arrangement which freed the young men to do their shopping and the ladies to exchange gossip. [8]

Self-reliance had been new to the young men, as each had always lived at home until this move to London; Jules's meagre life skills had run to using an iron to press a knife crease in his trousers; polish a mirror finish on his shoes and the ability to prepare the simplest food with the aid of a tin. City skills, you may think, but he was not as 'at ease' in the city as his friends; If asked, he would admit to being far happier in the countryside, walking through wild grass and surrounded by the sounds and works of nature.

He had one very special place; but he would not dare admit of his lone adventures there – his pale body exposed to and warmed by the kindly sun or caressing breeze. He had not even told his Sukie about that, but he had taken her there that summer and introduced her to his friends the inquisitive rabbits and the birds and the tiny bank voles. And in return she had told him the names of the wild flowers. And when they had run out of words to say, they had discarded all of their clothes and lay down together on a broad rabbit lawn – to travel in their own way, to the world no one else could share.

And afterwards, they bathed naked in the sun, while sparkling blue damselflies – distracted – ceased their own charming courtship to perch in pairs as living jewels on their hands, arms and shoulders.

In the City outdoors there is only the works of man and unyielding asphalt or concrete slabs underfoot; and the only free running water a flood from a fractured water pipe or an incessant drip from an overflow set on a building high above the street. And the only wild creatures; a drab and bedraggled sewer rat; a stray dog or two: feral cats; mice and foxes. All, it seemed to Jules, reduced in this alien environment to scavenging refuse in order to survive.

Jules's flatmate friends were far more at home in the City; Roger, an only child, loved everything about it, and, being full of ambition, could not wait to take advantage of the career opportunities which seemed to appear from around every corner – William in contrast, was far more easy-going; His parents were professional classical musicians and he and his two, or was it three, sisters could all play the piano well.

That was the one thing the three found missing from the myriad of shops along this street; a music shop with American guitars for Roger to admire or records for him to buy; and classical music for William to look through and some jazz records for Jules. There had been one here in the recent past, evidenced by Columbia, Decca and EMI logo's above a doorway, but Television was the big thing now and as Jules passed he saw that shop was now filled with smart receivers – 'Sets' left switched on and, deprived of any de-codeable transmission, lamely displaying floating 'snow' which Jules imagined was Cosmic energy left over after the creation of the universe or 'fall-out' from Hiroshima and Nagasaki.

The life force of so many lovers and the loved vaporised in an instant to float in the ether as Angels.

A distraction – an ambulance rushes at high speed across the next junction; Its flashing lights projecting sudden colour into the night and upwards to illuminate the mist swirling over the rooftops. Its only sounds are the urgent patter of its balloon tyres on the cobbled road surface and the whisper of its perfectly tuned engine. The traffic signals had displayed an insistent red light as it approached and to Jules's momentary surprise, and as it passes they continue to switch calmly and obediently through their well-rehearsed sequence … red … red and amber … green … amber … red; totally oblivious or uncaring of the vehicles blatant disobedience.

Jules always looks 'on the bright side' when he sees a speeding ambulance and he stands for a minute and waits to see if a car carrying the 'father to be' is in pursuit, but no car comes. Then, still optimistic, he attempts to track the vehicles progress by following the light from its flashing beacons, but it is quickly swallowed up, leaving him unsure whether it had entered the grounds of the nearby hospital. But he imagines it has, and a time in the future when his magical Sukie might be about to give birth to their child with him there to witness the miracle – and holding her hand.

Dancers

The Hercules tavern stands across the junction and as Jules passes it he is forced to step of the broad pavement and into the road to avoid crunching over broken glass and shattered bottles; reminders of why the Hercules 'Pub' is not to his or his friends' taste – Sure it is licensed for music and there is music, but when they'd called in – there had been no public dancing. Instead the largest room, which is decorated in High Victorian style with mock Corinthian columns, was crammed full of people – mostly men in their middle years; some standing against the walls, sitting tall on bar stools or standing on chairs – while others sit equally open mouthed on brown bent wood chairs set around small tables.

The attraction was two girls, each with her own tiny table which served as a stage for her dancing and a home for a large beer glass overflowing with paper money donated by an intoxicated, over excited and voiceful crowd.

The three young men had arrived when the dancers were already well into their routine and auctioning their panties; and the three students had quickly downed their 'halves' and left before the first girl had accepted a 'fifty' in exchange for that skimpy garment. An assumption made in response to the deafening guffaws and cheers which emanating from every window in the old building as they crossed over the junction to The Horse and Groom, to discover beer which was more to their taste; a darts board and – after another burst of rapturous applause from over the junction – welcome peace and tranquillity.

The event had made them recall, during a few rounds of darts and a glass or two of ale, their beloved art school and the many drawings they'd made from pretty life models who were mostly young women no older than themselves – or the two 'exotic' dancers over the road – and when the time came to return home they were full of respect for the girls' undoubted pluck. [2]

Uncle Pierre

With the Hercules safely passed there is now only a few hundred meters for Jules to walk to reach his bed in the Mansions, a walk punctuated by more familiar landmarks – the dark windows of the Dental practice; the second-hand furniture sale rooms; The Tobacconist; the Butchers; the Barbers and the Ironmongers – The last being a treasure house stocked from floor to ceiling with anything and everything one might wish for; and the proprietor a genial character of French descent in spotless brown coveralls and a pocketed apron. He has sold the friends, on their first ever shopping expedition, among other essentials, a set of cheap aluminium pans and two sets of duplicate keys for their maisonette.

Jules had wondered about this 'shop' because when he'd first gone to collect the keys, there had been no response to his repeated 'Hellos' and he'd cheekily wandered into the back and discovered, among more of the man's extensive and intriguing stock, a fine workshop with a couple of precision lathes and a milling machine, beside which were parts he recognised, from his short time in the Army Cadet Corps, as parts for or from a service revolver.

And after mentioning this to his flatmates, over a glass or two of beer, the three had created an imagined past for him as 'Pierre' a gunsmith working for the French résistance.

He was definitely an all right guy, because when they'd returned a few weeks later to buy, or borrow a bicycle spanner and a puncture repair outfit from him, the man had refused them outright, insisting that the machine must be repaired 'sans default' so only he should do the work 'without problem'. The rims, he insisted, must be checked and made true; and the spokes; and the frame; and the brakes; all must be 'parfait' – and faced with such overwhelming persuasion and the lack of a single tool forthcoming – they were obliged to capitulate.

And the charge made was little more than they had expected to pay for the tools and materials – so all were pleased – not least the old man who appeared overjoyed to add, to what must have been an already extensive collection of adoptee, a pretty young niece and three nephews. And he'd restored the bicycle as he'd promised; mechanically perfect, like the keys. It was clear the man loved his work; the complete opposite of the two much younger butchers who occupied the butchers shop next door who 'came over' as a rancid pair to match some of their produce. [10]

Detectives and Foxes

When he is abreast the barbers, Jules senses he is being watched and turns to look behind him, but there is no-one there or across the wide street where a glow from a cigarette has suggested a last chance to direct someone to the compassionate lady with the soup kitchen or the shelter of Waterloo Station.

However as Jules approaches he sees no homeless person, only a Riley Pathfinder car parked in the shadows, and he is about to return to the doorway of the Mansions when he notices the driver's window is wound down – and curious – he takes a few steps nearer, but is stopping dead in his tracks. There are people in the car; two men wrapped in thick outdoor clothing – one is smoking and letting his cigarette smoke exit through the window to mingle seamlessly with the surrounding fog – the other is writing in a note book. And on the cars walnut dashboard there is a light brown leather holster and a revolver which marks them as a couple of detectives from the nearby police station comparing notes before they go 'off shift'

And with that knowledge it is time for Jules to abandon his quest to find a homeless person, but before he reaches the mansions doorway his eye is caught by a lone and lean Fox; and as he's never seen one roaming in a city before, and only at distance in the countryside, he stops for a moment to admire it's lithe shape as it slinks in and out of the shadows; weaving it's insolent way south towards Lambeth Road and stopping occasionally to look back to 'stare out' Jules, until a distant 'Yelp' makes them both transfer their attention to two others on Jules's side of the road unified as only foxes can be.

And when Jules looks back to his fox, its head down posture seems to mirror his feelings a few days before when his Sukie had refused his kiss. And in an instant the policemen are forgotten so he might tell his fox, eye to eye, that he must do as he had done and, even if it risked ridicule, declare his love for her; tell her how much he loves her; tell her that his life would be empty without her; and, above all, that he will stand by her whatever. And with all that said, all would work out fine.

But his silent words, projected through the night, appear to be wasted on the creature, which turns its back on Jules to resume its sullen patrol southward until its image is swallowed completely by the chilling mist which is fast becoming a freezing fog.

The Mansions

The entrance hallway of this optimistically named building shares its style of decor with that of a Victorian prison or hospital, or the nearby Lambeth North Underground Station; with its walls lined with ceramic tiles; some carrying a moulded Art Nouveau leaf design in shades of green to separate plain tiles above from the decorative cream and green of the lower ones.

Beyond and above this far from cosy space, are twenty-three dwellings spread over three floors; each one a 'home' to someone Jules and his friends might never see, but have heard as they had passed through this amplifying echo chamber. However they know one is a musician, because a room above Jules's shares the same tiny atrium which has allowed Chopin nocturnes to float down to him in the evenings and Bach cantatas, equally sometimes, to herald the dawn.

Every sound resonates in this entrance space, and it does now, embarrassing Jules with its amplification of the ugly but unavoidable judder of the sagging door as he opens it; and, because he's forgotten that it is far less reluctant to close, the resulting deafening crash.

It is dark. Outside where there was street lighting and diffused moonlight, but here the entire space is 'lit' by a single dust covered bulb, of dubious power, which is hanging from a long and equally dust encrusted flex somewhere high above the first floor landing. But there is light enough for him to see, on his right, the broad staircase which leads to the upper floors with stone treads worn by over a century of traffic to be as smooth and polished as the hardwood banister; and to the left of this the dark corridor which leads to – who knows where – and on his left the unassuming door to his apartment which he opens as quickly as he can, unwilling to be associated with the dreadful crash which, he hopes, has not roused too many from their sleep.

Home at Last

Jules's room is two steps inside the outside door and to the left, opposite the one his friends share, and in front is a steep and narrow stairway which leads down to the living area with a kitchenette, beyond which, and directly beneath Jules's room, is a spacious bathroom with a water closet which can double as a photographic darkroom (It changes from one function to the other in just a few moments by placing, or removing a board jammed against the window).

Jules room is never totally dark as light from the musician's room, or the room above that, spills into it through his window; so he does not put on the light, instead he hangs his overcoat on the back of the door and part undresses in the half-light; throwing his tie and then his shirt onto the back of a chair placed near the foot of the bed for that purpose. His shirt, only part folded, lands perfectly, but then slides to the floor.

He recovers it; re-folds it; puts his shoes under the chair (he has only one serviceable pair) and then, being more careful, he replaces the shirt.

There are other clothes on the chair, slippery clothes – and there are shoes under it too – which create a second of uncertainty in which he wonders if he has entered the right door of the Mansions (There is an identical entrance a hundred metres or so nearer to the Hercules) and he looks around him.

To his right is an ancient over-ornate and battered wardrobe (in eighteenth century French style with a huge mirrored door) which looks quite like his; and it is standing in its proper place across that corner of the room. And to the left of it, and near the foot of a bed, is the chairdrobe (the old and elegant chair too fragile for anyone to contemplate sitting on) and to his left; a small bedside chest of drawers. And in the centre of the room a single bed is draped in a dull blue sculpted candlewick cover which brings to mind magical times with Sukie and a single time when it served as a setting for a photo-shoot and many portraits of another pretty girl and a wish then that he'd never tried to dye it blue, but had left it white. [11].

It is his room.

The shoes are quite small and when he holds one up to catch the faint light he can see it has a small heal, a rounded toe and a strap-over fastening. It would seem his friends have held a half-term party and a guest has left them behind and gone home in her party shoes. And when he kneels down to return it to its place, he finds she has left her day clothes behind too, which prompts him to take a second look at the bed. It is a far more careful look than before and it reveals a low, but distinct mound.

The left-over party girl has not gone home!

Such a discovery may have been a welcome one or the subject of a young man's dream for some; or for Jules if the mound had been his Sukie. But right now and for him it isn't. His only wish is to curl-up in his bed and to sleep soundly through the few remaining hours of night.

Jules's Madonna in Red

His first thought, which is really a wish, is that the intruder is Val, a nineteen year old fellow student who was at the same art school as him and had posed many times for portrait photographs. She has stayed at the mansions three, or even four times now and each time shared his bed. And they had slept at their ease – the girl because of the many times she had been his model and amused herself, between shots, by testing his natural improvised philosophy against her Christian beliefs – and he for her saying

'I believe that if the world belonged to you, it would be a truly safe and beautiful place.'

Words which followed a discussion about the dangers within collective conscience which had been triggered, curiously, by that days' news of still more bombing with 'agent orange' in Vietnam – touching 'on route' on the strange willingness of so many of their own parents' generation to project an imagined inbuilt moral degeneracy onto all of modern youth.

Their occasional association (not their sleeping together) had bemused some, if not all, of their fellow students who'd assumed Jules's ambition was not just to add to his growing portfolio of portrait photographs, but to bed her if he could (she was after all one of the college beauties – elegant and slim with lots of shiny dark hair with eyes to match – not to mention her legs which were the longest and best shaped on campus – but they 'knew' he had no chance – he'd even been a source of falling about laughter after one student dared to suggest, in loud conversation, that in the unlikely event of him enticing her between the sheets, her virgin status would be safe enough, because she could whisper at the critical moment '... Luke; ...chapter seven; Verse three.' or something similar, and poor old Jules's manhood would shrink away to a limp nothing in an instant.

Any old quotation would do.

The two, Val and Jules, overheard it, as was intended (they were sitting close-by discussing Jules making an impressive photograph based poster for the Christian fellowship of Students) and wishing the 'joke' might, or must, back-fire on the teasing group, Val had suggested a 'quotation' for Jules to suggest to them. And after she'd left to attend her afternoon classes he'd approached the men's table and said,

' ... Mm ... Luke seven ... verse three ... don't know that one ... but get this one ... what if she gasped, while laying naked and breathless, "Genesis twenty-nine".

The four had remained silent while Jules continued, asking

'Don't you know that one?' and continued, only slightly misquoting the verse with 'and he lay with her that night ... and came into her...''

It had been a sort of fun thing to do – and very 'sporting' of Val who must have known the idea of him ever entering her could never have crossed his mind – even when she'd shared his bed undressed down to the flimsiest and most delicately lace edged bra and pants, or, as she had been on one occasion, with those tiny items forsaken in favour of an equally, or even more transparent slip – they would never touch, even though those flimsy garments created no barrier to the eye or the faintest light hiding in half darkness. They were, like her belief in God, and the respect they shared for each other, unbreakable while being totally invisible.

Jules had wondered, from time to time, how she reconciled wearing such garments, with her perfectly virtuous mind, and had sometimes wondered if it might have been a test of his philosophy.

But that was something he would never know, as to ask her would have been an admission that, on at least one occasion, he'd peeped out from under the covers as she'd dressed, to admire in silent secret her fabulous nakedness; broken her trust; polluted their 'Utopia' where only their ideals; their 'perfect' ideas and their passionate philosophising might be allowed to touch; and excite; and intertwine.

So if the mound was her, all would be perfect, but on further examination it could not. *For a start the shoes are far too small. And her choice would have been for more stylish ones with proper heels. And the box-pleat skirt, on the chair back, would not be her choice either – even though the school girl 'look' is fashionable and 'everywhere' on huge posters advertising knee-high white boots.* [12] And in a moment it comes to him – He knows who the mound is – It is Juliet, or to be more accurate the girl who was to be 'Juliet' in his and William's planned four minute 16mm movie in celebration of being alive.

On Trial

They ... Jukes and William ... had chosen her, or she had chosen them, after they'd encountered her with a friend in Hyde Park.

It had been a warm sunny day and the two were, at first, were just walking and talking while sharing a small book; but suddenly they were running; stopping; turning; spinning;

laughing; filling the space between them with wonderful shapes and the whole world around them with joy. And both were beautiful, but she especially so because of the way she moved – dancing as she walked – floating, when she jumped in the air to deny the book from her friend, seeming as weightless as a feather in the wind. And to go with that charm, she had the face and the figure of an Angel. An Angel who, if she proved to be of this world, might be seventeen or a young eighteen, or at the very least a sophisticated sixteen, but to Jules's later consternation was younger still.

So now his welcome refuge from the cold is a minefield and its occupant a siren sent to provide a fast track – with only a short diversion via the local Magistrates' Court – to possible disgrace followed by a spell in jail and a once bright future destroyed.
He imagines the scene – the Chief Magistrate sitting aloof on the bench with her stone face exuding total contempt – and her two colleges sitting one to each side, equally, if not more, hard-faced. And, between those three and himself, the prosecutor, who looks much like an older version of himself, but of necessity, clean shaven.

His accuser turns to address him...
'... So ... Mister Jules Renard ...' (there is a sneering emphasis on the word Mister. '... You came home in the middle of that night, and just slipped into bed with her ... without a

second thought or a "by-your-leave" or a "thank-you-very-much" and slept with her? ...'

'Yes I did – but no – not without asking. And it was so dreadfully cold – how could I possibly have asked her to leave a warm bed and sleep down stairs?'

' .. so you did sleep with her ... a schoolgirl ... a fourteen year old girl ... and you were alone there together ... just sleeping ... until the morning.'

Jules did not like the man's clever tone or inference in the words '...until the morning', because he knows from 'sleeping' with Val that this might be – is always – the tricky time.

'Yes I did. We did'

' .. And you expect the Bench to believe you never touched her ... even though, on your own admission, it is a narrow bed ... A single bed ... A bed intended for just one?

'Yes I do. I sleep on the edge.'

There is a short silence in which Jules hopes his interrogator hasn't noticed the slip of his tongue.

'Have you ever kissed ... you and the pretty school-girl?

Shit – What does he know – and how? – Can I lie? No way – I'm on oath here – the Bible is just there laying there on the edge of the stand – its huge blind embossed cross catching the light and looking back at me – I will have to tell the truth, but as little as I must because he's going to love this answer

'Yes'

'And when was this?'

Oh God – dare I say? her drink was supposed to be Orange Juice, but later I hadn't been all that sure – anyway I didn't buy the drinks it was Roger, William and Lez who went to the Bar leaving me alone with her. But for now that doesn't matter – the underage drinking bit!

'We were on the decking – overlooking the River – behind the 'Prospect' – The Prospect of Whitby.

'In the moonlight ...?

How could he possibly know that – the moonlight bit?

'... and there was romance in the air ...?'

I can get out of this one

'Yes there was – the romance of the river – the hypnotic sound of water lapping against the shore and the voices of unseen lighter-men calling to each other through the mist – and the smell of smoke and steam mixed with oil; and the breathy comings and goings of the ghostly steam tugs – but between the girl and me and after the kiss – No chance.'

I shouldn't have said that – the after the kiss bit – or perhaps I should – I would have been happy just to stand and watch the ghosts of the tugs and listen to those sounds all night

'And why was this ...?'

This is going to be interesting – I should never of said 'No chance' but that first kiss was so unexpected and so passionate – And her second was one I will remember for the rest of time – a kiss from a siren which implored me to place my arms around her – and insist my brain

---

45

put aside all rational thought in favour of imagining making passionate love with her – an idea totally out of the question (whoever she might be) – unless of course, she was my Sukie and it was our wedding night.

But I can't tell them this. What might they think of her? It could defame my wonderfully bright and captivating friend – who I could so easily have fallen in love with – so I must play down the inexplicable power which flowed from her if I possibly can.

'... Well, your Honour, it was because the kisses she gave were far too passionate for me. And I told her, in reply to her scalding me for being a poor kisser that any man kissed like that would want to make love with her. And, as I loved another, I couldn't and mustn't return it. And I begged her not to kiss anyone in that way – ever -- especially when it was for the first time – it just wasn't safe.'

'... You told her that ...?''

'Yes – and in reply she told me she always kissed that way – that she'd practiced "a lot" with the boys in her class – and she thought I would like it as much as they did'

That would be a stupid thing to say – the 'want to make love with her' bit – even though it was true enough – hadn't every nerve in your body begged you to join in? And those lucky boys – they must have queued half way around the science block for kisses from her.

'... This is after you'd pushed her away?'

I had to do something – she was, with little more than a touch of her lips, flooding my heart and other parts of my body with impossible ideas.

'Yes your Honour – but I didn't push her – I gently lifted her arms from around my neck and held them between us to keep us apart.

It was then that I dared to ask how old the boys were and she'd answered – without as much as a moment's hesitation – "The same as me" and when I pressed and asked what that might be she told me.'

'So you knew from that time onward that the girl was a Minor ... below the age of consent ... a child?'

God, I wish he hadn't used the word 'Child'.

'Yes your Honour but honestly before she told me – I couldn't have known – no man could have. Sure I'd guessed she might be under eighteen – but she was so confident in her manner – and when I explained that a man could go to Jail – she laughed, I think – I hope – with joy at her being mistaken for eighteen and not for being 'Jail-bait' – and then, as if to make things worse for me, she said I should have seen her, on the previous Friday afternoon, playing hockey on the sports field in her navy gym tunic – I would have believed she was fourteen then.'

What had I said? This would be the picture the Magistrates would have of her now – most likely with the embellishment of knobbly knees and her hair done-up in bunches – so you might as well give-up any idea of waking her – or of sleeping beside her, because if you don't you might as well resign yourself, this moment, to ruin after a spell in Jail.

'... and then ...?'

'The others arrived with the drinks ... and we were entertained by Lez's colourful stories about the pub – that it was named 'Prospect' after an old sailing ship from Whitby which used the staithe nearby. And some grizzly story about a Gibbet – which we all had to risk falling into the river to see. After which we talked about our flat-warming party – it was planned for the next weekend – and because Will' had canvassed the other tenants in the Mansions, could continue into the small hours – or through the night – if we wished'

'And you invited the girl?'

'Not really your Honours – not me – she kind of invited herself. You see, Lez had taken the incomplete guest list from William – and insisted there weren't anything like enough women on it – and as I hadn't had a chance to tell them how young she was – he added her. But it wasn't going to be a Pyjama party or anything of that sort. It was to be – good music – good company – a few drinks – snacks – that kind of thing – a 'get to know each other' evening for everyone in our post-dip year who might wish to come – some of whom were high achieving graduates from overseas. There would be no shortage of conversation.'

'...So ...'

I really must look-up how to address the Bench properly. I'll be calling them 'Your Majesties' next.

'And with that done we all piled into Lez's old Wolseley and he drove us to another riverside pub, this time on the south of the river, where, according to him, Wren hung out living on Jellied Eels while supervising, at distance, the building of the dome for St Paul's – we dropped 'Juliet' at London Bridge Station on the way – she said she could get a train to South Woodford from there – She lives in South Woodford.'

'And when you left her at the station you kissed her good night'

'Yes; I kissed her goodnight, but this time on the cheek. And as she walked up the ramp towards the station, I thought she'd taken notice of what I'd said earlier. And then my heart sank, because she hadn't gone very far up the ramp before she turned and skipped back to say "I'll bring a nightie." and before I'd realised the inference of it and composed myself, she'd gone.'

To tell anyone this would not be a good idea. And why – in the name of heaven – did you ever think of saying 'skip' you idiot?

'... and did she come to the party?'

'Yes – and, as I'd feared – with coral lipstick and all – she looked even less like a girl of fourteen and for a little while I tried to keep Lez away from her – he'd been flirting with her at the 'Prospect' and I'd had no chance to warn him. But it ceased to be a problem when he was charmed to distraction by the serene Viveka, a stunningly beautiful, but, up until then, very shy Swedish student and 'Juliet' had, in her turn, became engrossed listening to Aspen's charming voice describing his native Norway – until ...'

'Until?'

'It was about ten – I went to find her to remind her it was nearing the time she should be going home – But I couldn't see her and, assuming she was in the bathroom or similar, I slipped into my room to get the title frame designs for our film, as a few of our guests wished to see them – especially Hillary as I had used her favourite type-face 'Perpetua', with only a little modification, for the single title word.'

'... and she was in your room... your Juliet?'

'Perhaps she was, or she was going there. It was in use as a cloakroom-come-changing room for the female guests, because of the big mirror on the wardrobe door – there were clothes everywhere – the bed was stacked high with them ...'

You shouldn't have mentioned the bed!

'... and because the floor was littered with shoes and bags and stuff I turned the light on so I wouldn't fall over them. But in less than a second it went out.'

'... She'd turned off the light?'

I don't know – And don't try and make me say things which might suggest stuff!

'I don't know – I turned to check the switch – it's an 'ancient' thing – probably dating from the days of Direct Current – and I'd assumed had gone 'high-resistance' like it does – You have to turn it on and off a few times to clean the contacts and it works again – it's one of the reasons I don't use the light much – because of the sparks – and the smell of burning metal. And she was there – standing in the doorway – so I suppose she could have.

    I was taken by surprise because, wearing white lace, and back-lit by light from the doorway, she looked for the entire world like a ghost. And when she said she had 'cum' to me – and that I had 'cum' to her and it was time for some kissing lessons – Honest – it was unreal, especially with her doing her 'Cathy' bit and making fun of my vowels – but before I could join in her game – her play-acting – by retaliating with a 'Heathcliff' impression' I remembered her party dress was pale blue.'

    Why am I telling them all this?

'... And this is how you knew she was Juliet, because she was not wearing a blue dress?'

    No stupid – but she'd been at the flat all day helping get stuff ready in just her underwear – so she wouldn't spoil her 'best dress'. It was nothing to her, but we'd noticed – what man wouldn't

    Perhaps I should tell them this – so they might know it was no 'big deal for her.

'... It was when she gave-up on the silly dialect ...'

    I mustn't tell anyone that I'd let her take off my tie – and unbutton my shirt – and pull it out of my waistband before its double cuffs and my tight cuff-links saved the day.

'... and there was the welcome sounds of female laughter – Veka and some others were coming up the stairs ...'

That's good – using the word 'welcome'

' ... And the door opened suddenly then closed – followed by charming giggled apologies – Veka has the best giggle I've ever heard – it's her accent – followed by requests for us to hand out, to the excited disembodied voices, poorly described items of clothing.

It put an end to her playing, but in that brief moment; when the light spilled through the door; I caught sight of our combined reflection in the wardrobe mirror – her long slender back – those hips and her lovely bottom – magnificent – the anatomy of a goddess to rival that of the Rokeby Venus.'

I shouldn't have let that thought in – the beauty of her body – they might imagine I'd given way to temptation and begun to lust after here – There is a saying – 'when you've dug a hole for yourself – you should stop digging'. So stop digging.

'The bench is intrigued Mr Renard ... pray continue.'

Perhaps I've got away with the Rokeby Venus bit ... Did I say that!

'It was too late for public transport – so while she dressed and collected her things together, I nipped out and telephoned for a black-cab to take her home – from the phonebox outside the ironmongers – There isn't a rank in Kennington Road.'

'And you went with her ...'

'Yes, of course, I wanted to be sure she got home safe and sound.'

Yes – that's better – make it sound as if you're behaving like an older brother or a cousin or something – and when you do speak – you must say less. For instance you mustn't tell their Worships any detail of the journey – About the girl telling you about her friends reading sections of 'Lady Chatterley's Lover' to each other, and confiding to you her urgent wish to experience the turbulent magic which dissolved the soul of Lady Chatterley and 'made her woman'.[13]

Telling anyone this would compromise her – even though it would give you a chance to tell them of your remonstrations with her to give up that dangerous quest and share with them your fear that she and her friends; two of whom (she'd confided) had already given their maidenhood away to Bancroft's Boys, (whoever they might be) for nothing, might, if they persisted in their quest, be 'taken', not so much for the free-thinking 'moderns' they believed they were, but considered 'an easy lay' and 'cheap'.

And with that argument put aside, she might succeed in her quest and 'become woman', whatever that might mean, but did she really want that? She should know just how unbelievably charming she is now (almost as much so as Sukie) – she mustn't do anything to 'spoil' that – whatever.

But, above all you mustn't admit that making love with her had crossed your mind, fearful that if you didn't she would continue her quest and expose herself to dangers she could not imagine; violence; rape; an unwished for child by a careless man (or a boy) and a bright future sacrificed without a hint of Lady Chatterley's beguiling metamorphosis.

'...and during the journey ...?'

'I can't 'tell' on her, it could ruin her future'

' ... There were no kissing lessons, if that's what you mean; we just talked of this and that, but mostly about her future and that of her close school-friends. And before you ask again – Yes we kissed goodnight and because it was to be for the last time – I allowed a little of her magic to enter and charm me.

That was good – apart from the last bit, but – come on – when you were in the taxi, and trying to convince her to stay a virgin, you'd imagined her as Sukie – that they were her hands you were holding then – and when you were standing beside the taxi saying, what was to be our last goodbye, they were her soft lips – Sukie's lips – which tasted as ripe and as glamorous and as forbidden as stolen raspberries

And it's a pity you can't say that your driver had enjoyed overhearing your ardent remonstrations so much that he insisted you paid only half the fare to South Woodford and waved all the return fair as a thank-you for what he'd called 'a wonderful treat' adding that he'd never believed a young man could work so hard at getting out of having sex with his girlfriend – and her such a pretty one too.

'Did you see her again?'

' No – she's Roger's girlfriend now – I telephoned her mum to let her know the very next day – It was a cultured female voice which answered – quite posh really – and when I asked if it was Mrs A – the voice said it was.'

But she didn't confirm it either, you fool.

There is a short silence before the prosecutor asks – incredulous

' .. So this is why you thought you would get into bed with her? And get away with it – Because she wasn't your girlfriend anymore, but Roger's?'

Now he's being really sarcastic – and I've probably dropped Roger in it now so you're not going to get off without telling at least some of the other stuff.

But he's quite right; she's most likely given up on me now and we might sleep side by side and not touch – just like with Val – and all will be well.

And it is with this idea, and only a little fear of being woken by a kiss, Jules's trial is adjourned – awaiting further evidence.

His new plan, if plan it is, is to waken her 'accidentally' by throwing his clothes on the bed and making more noise than usual as he completes getting ready for bed – and when she is safely eased from her slumber he will either ask her to sleep elsewhere, perhaps in Roger's bed if they are still together, or ask if he might share.

And he does make a lot of noise, some of it unintentional when he falls over her bag and spills some of its contents onto the floor – a tiny box of pills included. But his sleeping Venus's only response is to temporarily destroy Diego Velázquez's tantalizing silhouette to form another with its disturbing charm multiplied by ten.

But Jules believes she could be part awake now and he dares complete his dressing for sleep close by her bedside – shivering – with goose-bumps forming on every part of him – not only because of the cold air in the room, but because from here the pattern of her hair, against the crisp white of the pillow, is too much like Sukie's when it framed her face after their very first time.

'Shhhhhh' he whispers, forcing himself to return to the present and the task in hand, 'Please wake up – just a little – Please.'

And when 'Venus' does wake that 'very little' he continues in an even softer tone,

'It's only Jules ... please don't be frightened – all I want is to sleep – honest.'

She moves again – and a small hand appears to uncover her face – and she turns towards him and opens her eyes. He is close to her now and he can see they are sleepy brown eyes, which, as they focus and recognise Jules, communicate to him a vision of perfect contentment.

He might have woken her from a dream of finding him there.

And as if in concert with that idea Jules's previous hardened resolve to turf out the trespasser is extinguished – gone in a moment – he can't evict her – all he can do as his weary mind soars free of sleeping with a fourteen year old and the possibility of ending up in Jail, is say

'Wendy ... please can I come in?' spoken words which are followed by a torrent of silent questions:-

But why? ... What are you doing here? I know you once asked ... and it was so very flattering ... and still is ... But I didn't say you could ... and anyway ... if I was to believe half the things you've said, you should be far away from London now and safe from harm ... Or was all of that.... and the rest.... a cruel fantasy... a make-believe to break my heart?

His spoken thoughts are less complex and less confrontational

'... It's so very cold out here ... and it is my bed after-all ... and I would love to sleep in it. Honest, all I want is to sleep. I know it's an awful lot to ask ... but could you ... would you please move-over and let me in?'

A few moments pass before she makes a sleepy smile followed by an inviting wriggle towards the far side of the bed. And with his heart pounding – he knows not why, but it could be him noticing how unbelievably 'good' his benefactor looks wearing his best pyjama top – he accepts the unspoken and slides in beside her, taking great care not to push his way in, or to

touch, or to pull any of the blissfully warmed
and fragranced sheets from over his friend.

And when he is settled, laying perched
on the edge of the mattress with his back to her
and his heart is quieter, he whispers

'Thank you so much ... See you in the
morning.' And in reply she whispers in her turn

'Good night Jules' and he

'Good night Wendy sweet dreams'

But that look in her eyes had been so
trusting and so much like Sukie's before, during
and after their 'IT', he imagines it is she who is
lying beside him and he adds silently

'My darling Sukie ... I love you.' And
then after closing his eyes so he can imagine her
more vividly, he recalls the time when he
discovered his Sukie was supernatural.

A dream of Sukie...

It took almost an hour for the number fifty-three
bus to cover the fifteen or so miles to the Art
School; ample time for them to talk and become
friends or just sit together quietly. It was her
easy manner, pretty face and gentle eyes – in
which sparkling tears would appear for no other
reason than to captivate – which did the rest.
And now, even after nearly two years of
adventuring together, if anyone had asked them
to describe their relationship the two might still
say 'friends', or 'good friends' because what
happened between them was, as far as they
knew, something unique to them and impossible
to name or compare with anything other people

might have experienced or imagined; not even in 'their wildest dreams.'

In the language of the day it was 'something else' ... or just 'else'. An 'Else' which had begun at a fancy dress dance where Sukie and her two special girlfriends, Sue and Tansy had dressed as 'Flappers' in full and convincing period dress and hairstyles. Sukie's was home-made with a little help from her mum who'd donated yard upon yard of fine silk fringing and three very long necklaces of coloured glass and amber beads.

She looked amazing and Jules had monopolised her and her friends all the evening – all three laughing at Jules's inept attempts to 'do' the Charleston, which prompted him to protest his preference for 'Rock and Roll' and it was late – time for Sukie to leave so she might catch the last bus home and they were briefly alone in the cloakroom – when they kissed.

Jules had expected a simple thank you touch – to be over in a moment – but when their lips meet for that moment there is so much more – a surprising excitement passes to waken every nerve in his body and demand an experiment – a repeat of the touch.

It is a very pleasant surprise and in the next few minutes, as they kiss, pause, and then kiss again, he suspects she can feel everything he is feeling and read every thought which has slipped unguarded into his head – because, between each brief touch she is taking those sensations and ideas and returning them to him magnified ten fold.

She is becoming, with each successive kiss, more and more enchanting.

And it is with bold ignorance, tempered with fear that she might read too much of his thoughts and be alarmed, that when their lips touch again, he has pressed himself very softly against her, to create – unknowing until that kiss – a new thrilling path through which to share the power of her electricity.

Their 'dared' closeness had been 'a first' for Jules and because of his friend's response – her 'beauty' and her naturalness he knew it must have been hers too. And a few days later, with boundaries understood, but unspoken, they continued their adventure – but this time it was in the privacy of Jules's tiny rented room – and as they had no word for what they had done at the dance, or what they might do then (doing sex being out of the question) they called it 'It'. [14]

And in that safe seclusion the two laid down together and Jules rubbing gently against her – her eyes saying 'I trust you.' and his, 'I've never known anyone quite like you', while concealing the truth that his every move was an experiment, only the proof of rightness the quickening of her heartbeat and the increased bliss in her eyes.

Several times, Jules had feared the intensity of her pleasure might harm her and he would stop, but in a moment or two she would breathe again and ask him, silently with her eyes, to continue.

It had been exhausting that first time; holding himself above her for so long, but his reward was beyond any possible imagining or comparison – to see and share her joy as each long wave of pleasure built upon the last – touching and then caressing every nerve as it passed to fill her eyes with ten thousand or more tiny shimmering tears of ecstasy – all of this until there was room for no more and her slender body arched itself, as if asking for a last touch, to curve upward again and then again as the flood passed, soothing her, caressing her, and then reluctantly allowing her to be still – to lie still and serene – her eyes still locked with his in shared disbelief.

It should have been enough for them both, but the lights in Sukie's eyes which had guided the inexperienced Jules was still there; holding his gaze – one moment showing him a myriad of tiny dancing rainbows and in the next a thousand minute emerald green stars – then flickering bright and warm sunshine. And still further and deeper into her, through what had been – when she was a mere mortal – the darkest part of her eyes; she shows him endless space filled with colourful spinning galaxies – spirals of stars and planets – some with tiny moons – and beyond those and even deeper within his incredible friend – an alternative Planet Earth with clouds and sea and sky and closer still – at ground level and surrounded by trees – a green meadow bathed in light to share and call their own.

It is a place filled with love, soft colours and birdsong – a place he wants to be – and with that wish he sees himself and Sukie walking there hand in hand and naked – and because they are naked he knows they must be in a kind of paradise – or they have accidentally discovered Heaven – Sukie's inner heaven. [15]

And accompanying that shared idea sunlight enters the room for the first time [16] caressing his friends face and creating an aura on the pillow which reflects around the room, filling it with light. And Jules, still absent in paradise, believes the light must be emanating from his friend and she is being made an Angel – and when his eyes adjust to the glare she has closed her eyes leaving some of her special tears lying sparkling on her cheeks – and he dares to kiss them away – one by one – wishing with each touch that a little of her magic might be enshrined in them and be transferred to him. They taste as sweet as honey – and after the third kiss, or the fourth, he feels sleepy and lies down at her side, and hooking a little fingers with her's he lets his own eyes close.

In mid-afternoon they wake into a material world outside of Sukie. And to Jules's dismay, fear and delight, Sukie is still, for the most part, in her Angel state, but working hard to re-learn the skills associated with being mortal – She has already mastered the art of not projecting excessive light everywhere; can speak using audible and charming sounds, instead of the silent language of Angels; and is practising other skills like standing and walking without falling over.

And Jules can feel his own arms again; his everyday thin ones which allow a maximum of twenty or so push ups before they threaten to explode with pain. And with that realisation he knows he has experienced a great secret. [17]

And later – after strong coffee – they walk hand in hand the half kilometre back to College, all the while trusting that when they arrive, no one would have noted their combined absence, or would have the knowledge required to know, or guess, the reason for Sukie's extraordinary serenity.

They needn't have worried as everyone else was hard at work and she was able to negotiate the long and over-polished walkway, which skirted the sculpture hall, and climb the steep and narrow stairs that led to room eleven without a single incident. [18]. It was here she spent the next hour or so with her, still occasionally disobedient, legs safely folded beneath her while her mortal head and hands attempted to co-operate with each other to transfer a fabric design she had prepared in the morning onto a silk screen.

Sukie's response to Jules's attentions that day had thrilled him – his young friend sharing herself in that way – entrusting him, with every single part of herself, so they might both be free to enjoy such a magical journey – and to such an amazing and unexpected destination. For him it had been a wonderful thing – a great privilege which brought with it a great responsibility – For he had introduced Sukie to sensations which, if shared with another man, might create in him only a desire for self-indulgence or selfish satisfaction.

And the weeks and months pass; and Jules and Sukie dance and kiss with others – Jules all the while fearing for his friend – but not one girl is anything like his Sukie and Sukie finds no one quite like Jules, so they find themselves drawn together again and walking and talking in the park or the botanical gardens, or just strolling in the town, where total strangers would mistake them for lovers and confront them with smiles and wish them a happy future together.

It had caused them both to wonder if they were 'in love', and Jules would thank them while Sukie suppressed giggles – not always with total success – and the next day, or the day after that, the two would give way to that crazy idea and find themselves, without a word spoken – in case that act might break the electricity – back in Jules's cosy room exploring more flower-strewn paths and sunlit glades.

Jules re-lives all of this in his sleep – for he is sleeping now – only waking from time to time to wonder at his amazing past good fortune and to recall yesterday, when in an attempt to understand his feelings for Sukie and his desire to be forever with her – he'd talked at length with his blinded father, whom he trusts as a friend and a man of science, and concluded Sukie was indeed a phenomenon – and at the dance – the prettiest capacitor [19] and the most elegant – living – laughing and giggling electrical generator there could ever be. [20]

And this decided; they had created a scene together, in which the slender Sukie is

dancing the art school bop – spinning and turning – her slender arms raised over her head intertwining with those of the ghost of Coulomb – who's pellucid body is attempting to combine with hers – sliding first this way, and then that, in it's attempt to follow her pretty gyrations – or in pursuit of her beads, which, as their wearer reversed and reversed again, passed over each other created a myriad of tiny sparks which danced through and around them like Fairy dust.
[21]

It had been, Jules believed, an enchanting scene for his blind father to 'see' even though it had partly destroyed his own imaginings of Sukie as a unique supernatural.

Jules's Bedfellow

Wendy, who lays contented beside him, is a student – at the same college as Jules – who has been kind enough to pose for him to take portrait photographs.

The brief was to create three press advertisements to promote a quieter Britain and Jules had chosen her for her natural looks; able to be 'taken' for a 'blue stocking'; a librarian; a smart shop assistant; a young 'mum', or a student – a girl naturally attractive without make-up and with a simple hairstyle. And she had posed, close-up, with one finger placed across her slightly open lips saying 'Shhhhhh'.

It had, he believed, been a good idea and Roger had complained that Jules's photographic prints of her, pasted-to-dry on the glass of their

French windows, had made him speak in a whisper – praise indeed – and proof to Jules that even if he was unsuccessful in the competition, his simple idea was effective and his choice of model perfect.

Jules had 'discovered' her in the student's common room and coffee bar; a huge space that occupied most of the north side of the sixth floor of the college tower block. She was sitting and talking with friends near the centre of the room and even at a distance he could see she was just right – so he'd simply walked over to her, and when a lull in the conversation allowed, he'd asked if she would be kind enough to be his Shhhhhh girl, by quickly explaining the project and his idea.

'Like this' she'd said, putting a finger to her lips and assuming the perfect pose

'Yes exactly like that, and with no more make-up than you have now apart from perhaps the tiniest bit of lipstick,' then after a second thought, 'No … not even that'

' ... 'Really?'

'Yes you are perfect just as you are. Please if you will do it for me, could you clear it with your teacher … or I can if you wish ... we will need about an hour or so … on Thursday afternoon? … straight after lunch?'

'I'm sure it will be O.K., but I will ask my teacher… It's Maths anyway, so I won't mind. It's a subject I can do, but not my favourite ... Just come to my classroom when you're ready... room sixteen'.

Jules was delighted with her. She was not only natural in appearance but in her manner. He could not have wished for better and had turned to leave, but was stopped by the girl asking;

'What should I do with my hair?'

Jules turned and looked at her again; scanned her well-defined features, admired the arrangement of a few attractive softly defined freckles on the left of her forehead, which strayed onto the bridge of her nose and across onto her cheek on that side. He hadn't noticed them before and suddenly he worried about them making her look childlike, but then he loved them, knowing them to be an asset as they gave another slant to his idea; another interpretation of her as a school girl wishing for quiet to do her homework. Her hair, which he was supposed to be looking at, was simply arranged, short and curved inward and forwards at the sides. And she has a fringe, through which he could just see those charming freckles, defined by a clip on black velvet bow. The style suited her face, with those big eyes, perfectly

'Nothing at all; could it be like it is now? Honestly you don't have to change one thing, just be you'

'Yes, if that's what you want' she said, hesitating a little; not believing that anyone would want to photograph her or anyone as they looked every day. 'Don't models make up and dress up for photographs'?

That had been that; He'd not even asked the girl's name, which he regretted when he turned up at her classroom not knowing who to ask for. But all was well, for as soon as he entered the room, the girl was up from her chair and quickly next to him, looking brilliant; wide eyed and beautiful. She was not really the plainish Jayne he had chosen. This girl had her dark hair piled up on top of a small but perfectly shaped head; a fringe curled over her forehead, its strands flowing from under a large soft velvet bow to touch her strong eyebrows; and her eyes are large and green.

It is a surprise, but also too late to do anything ... and anyway it might offend. You can't seem to criticise ... look a gift horse in the mouth.

'Is everything OK? ' he asks, thinking 'This (she) is some gorgeous gift horse'. His eyes are switching quickly between her, the turned heads of the entire class, and the teacher.

'Yes, Miss doesn't mind ...' she said brightly, making a point of flashing her eyes into his as she flounced past him saying '... but all the other girls are dead jealous'.

Jules, surprised, makes a long distance, 'thank you' to the lady teacher (it is mouthed rather than spoken) and she looks back at the twenty year old realising she hadn't had a chance to ask the girl if she would like someone, perhaps one of the other girls, or even herself to go with her – for proprieties sake – and she opens her mouth to speak, but she doesn't make a sound – instead her face reveals a belief that, if she was honest to herself, she would know the girl's likely answer. It would be the one she would have given if in her place – 'No thank you miss.'

The photographic studios are high in the tower block and the one Jules has 'booked' was, he had been told, on twelve-A. It is really the thirteenth, but the architect must have been superstitious – so it is the mezzanine of a two story deep twelfth only visible from outside the building as an extra deep floor – a design element which made finding the studio or any usable space in that part of the half-finished building a real adventure for the pair., especially as the cargo lift, the only one which stopped at both even and odd numbers, was not in commission, or was out of use.

In fact, the two soon gave up looking for any specific studio and 'crashed' one which had a space among the clutter. [22]

The session went superbly well, even better than he could have imagined – her face was perfect for the camera and her hands were small – by luck rather than any good management, because he'd been so 'smitten' by her face he'd forgotten her hand would be right at the front of the shot.

They talked too and, as part of his answers to her questions and vice-versa they revealed a little about themselves. She had never seen a camera quite like his Edixa before and wanted to know all about it – how he'd learned so much about photography – why he was using what she called 'the long black lens', instead of the short silver one the camera had when he first took it out of the hold-all bag – and had it all been awfully expensive? – In his replies he admitted the outfit hadn't been cheap, but had been fortunate enough to have support from his parent and prize money for college work which he'd used to buy some of the extra bits like his favourite lens for portraits – the black Japanese made one-three-five telephoto he was using now.

And although he was in the company of another girl, or because of that, he told her about his Sukie – how they had met more than two years earlier at art school and had, over time, become 'inseparable' but without any detail – as an aside to relax his model, so she might not feel threatened – after all the were alone together in a remote unvisited thirteenth floor studio.

Jules knew, as he took shot after shot, that there would be little to choose between the many exposures; her eyes were a tiny bit wider in one – that pretty strand of stray hair in a slightly different place in another – her finger a little closer to her lips in that one – the lighting a little softer in another – each negative a testament to these details.

And Wendy understood, so the two became friends; and unwitting confidants in those two hours and as the session progressed she told him she was only at this school for a short time; that she was giving evidence at a trial.; that it was all a great and grave secret and one she mustn't 'tell' about – but she would be able to pose for more pictures if he wanted. And he, pleased as punch at the girls' eagerness to pose and follow his prompts so willingly and perfectly, didn't listen to a single detail of what she said – Instead he encouraged her to take another minutely different pose, and spoke softly about his hopes for his future with Sukie. And in return, and perhaps encouraged by the confidentiality implied by the pose, she spoke of disturbing events in her childhood and more recent past – But he only half listened.

Then the building fell strangely silent and the camera did too – emptied of all unexposed film.

They had taken thirty-six careful portrait shots that afternoon: interspersed with lessons in photography – or with moving lights – or just becoming closer confidants – or changing lenses – or laughing at anything and everything to break the tension created by her spoken confidences.

But more shots were needed, in colour this time, so they agreed to meet on the same day and time in the following week – Wendy (Jules is now not sure it is her real name) would have finished her 'exams' by then – 'exams' Jules thought, was a word she'd used to describe the secret things she was involved with – So they agreed the 'date' and Jules thanked her for her promise of next week – and for being such a truly wonderful model and they were back in the doorway of her classroom in just a few minutes.

They found it empty apart from the teacher, who was ploughing through what appeared to be a mountain of papers on her desk, so Wendy sneaked across the room to collect her basket and when back in the doorway wished her teacher 'goodnight' and when the teacher looked up to see her, she placed a surprise kiss on his cheek and, although surprised, he stuck to his rehearsed script to thank the teacher for the loan of her charge, and in return she thanked him for returning her student safely – but the look on her face suggested another truth – it said 'I can guess from Wendy's eyes, what you might have been doing and I wish it could have been with me'.

Jules developed the film that same evening – in the bathroom at the Mansions – and each negative was as Jules expected – with the first few, as always, a little stiff and awkward. But it would be difficult to select from the remaining ones, other than by a process of elimination; but some could be rejected outright because of tiny black pin prick marks in her eyes which betrayed the tiny tears which had formed when she was either confiding too much to Jules or when she had laughed at his purposely inept attempts to explain the light meter, lens stops, shutter speeds and the meter that measured the light energy reflecting or was it radiating from her.

It was the word 'réciprocité' and Jules's purposely poor attempt to explain it. He had been thinking of the film, as he always did, as a living thing – an extension of himself– insisting '… the amount the film is exposed (to you) … must be neither too little, nor too much. Only then will the magic work'.

They both knew as he had laughed and she had giggled, that their own réciprocité was working perfectly.

Prints from those negatives were made here too, using an old (rescued from a junk shop) single condenser enlarger which was minus a lens until Jules adapted it to use one from his camera; and with this done and an inline switch spliced into a long lead, it quickly became a usable set-up. [23]

The prints were good, all things considered, and Jules was looking forward to taking the final one in colour, but when he arrived to collect his model, she wasn't there and no one – not even her teacher – seemed to know where she was, or wouldn't say. All he was able to discover was that she had been in some form of accident and that he shouldn't worry because she wasn't badly hurt and would soon be back.

It was bad news for Jules, because, apart from anything else, he'd come to like the girl and didn't expected any secrecy to extend to him. The only answer he could solicit was. 'Sorry; you will just have to wait. No doubt she will tell you all about it when she returns'.

Wendy's Accident

Three weeks had passed and Jules had resigned himself to the idea that he would never see his model again, and would have to abandon his project, when she waved to him across the common room; prompting him to run across the intervening space – dodged through the crowd – skirting dangerously around tables filled with plates of food and vulnerable cups of coffee – but he cared nothing for that, he was preoccupied – delighted to see her and her smile, but also calculating time and wondering if she would still be willing to continue as his model.

He imagined, as he got closer and she walked a few steps towards him, that she had a slight limp, but her face looked as perfect as ever – and she hadn't changed her hairstyle one bit either – She even had the same velvet bow in her hair –All that remained was the question – would she still be willing to pose for that last photograph? – The single exposure that would allow him to complete their entry to the competition.

'What happened?' he is breathless – his eyes scanning her face. And then their eyes meet and an unspoken understanding passes that communicates far more than the honest truth embedded in the softly spoken and inadequate words that followed

' ... I've been really worried about you; I've asked everyone ... everyone about you, and they told me you were away because you'd been in an accident ... on your bike?'

'Yes, that's true…I have been; and it ... the bike is broken ... its gears don't change anymore ... and the front wheel is really bent.'

'And you?' Jules asked softly looking into her large eyes – letting them ask the question.

And she holds his gaze and turns to face him, swivelling and pulling her knees up to place both her feet on the cushion between them – and looks down to invite him to look, saying – asking.

'Are you any good at punctures?'

Jules glanced down; the hem of centre panel of her skirt is draped over her knees and the side pleats are like curtains at each side. They are pretty knees; narrow and neat and without a blemish; and below them are prettily shaped bare legs and white bobby socks pulled over small feet.

She had discarded her shoes and for a moment he wondered what it was she wished him to see and then she opened her knees, revealing the insides of her upper thighs, and he knows.

They are covered in a multitude of bruising which extended as far as his eyes could see; the darkness of the black or blue, darker here and a little less there, but accentuated where they meet the pure bright white of new, prettily-edged, cotton under which all seems to extend.

He knew then what it was she wished him to know and their eyes meet. And at that moment they are so close they might be the only people in the room. It is a privacy which allowed him to whisper,

'Oh Wendy .... ' the rest, being so deeply felt and quietly spoken the words do not create a sound, but he asked her, through her eyes, 'please tell me... share it with me ... let me take away the hurt?'

A group crash and bash their way past them, waking Jules from his trance to see the girl's knees are still wide apart. And he says quietly, but a little too abruptly,

'Please don't do that ... show yourself like that ... to me ... to everyone ... to anyone'. He is looking around in panic, but she is as calm as calm could be and doesn't move an inch, so – in self-preservation – he moves even closer to give her the privacy he wishes for her, and continues, whispering a torrent of regret, should she have thought him abrupt or uncaring; adding

'... Someone ... anyone could have seen me looking.... What would they ... those other people think? ... I'm not even your boyfriend'. And, with this said, he looks around the room again. There is no-one who might see.

He might have continued with - 'Do you have no shame?' but he didn't get the chance because instead of closing her knees, which he'd hoped she would, she took hold of his right hand with both of hers and, opening her knees even further, she puts it gently against her and over one of the larger bruises.

'Feel how tender and swollen it is.' She is looking into his eyes and pressing his hand against her – his hand – which is moving in perceivably nearer to the top of her leg – and it is only a centimetre or two away from the white cotton when Jules realises and checks its progress.

And there is stillness in which a million questions pass between them and are answered in complete silence.

Only then does he remove his hand from under hers. And with that done his mind slips into overdrive, if not panic, because he realises what she had invited him to do – and what he has done:-

'OK - so she's been cruelly hurt, but that's no excuse ... she shouldn't have done that to me ... show herself in that way ... and as for putting my hand up her skirt... I'm a bloke for Gods sake ... what will people think - She's behaving like a slut.' But he thinks again; re-interpreting the open almost pleading look in her eyes, 'No ... it's not a bit sluttish... it's far more like the action of a child ... open and innocent ... as if she's asking me, in the only way she can, for help. Trusting ... But doesn't she understand ... It's O K for her to trust me, but there is no one else who will ... I'm just another student here ... and could be slung out on my ear for this ... or less ... and my future...the only one I care about, with Sukie, will be in ruins?

And he looks around the room, in panic, to see if anyone is staring at them in disbelief, but to his relief most of the students have left and, of the handful which remain, none are looking their way. But there is a man in a dark suit standing over by the door who is looking. And his look is straight at them, but all he would be able to see of the girl would be her head and shoulders. And the thought that he might have –

got away with it – allows Jules to speak another thought

'Oh, but Wendy … dear Wendy … it must have hurt'.

But he is not thinking of her being in a bicycle crash; because he has been in one – at a speed of nearly forty miles per hour – and he wasn't hurt like this, even though he'd hung onto the bars of the heavy machine as it tumbled over and over, giving him a severe bashing on the road; the cycles cross-bar; and the saddle.

'Yes, It ... what happened ... hurt a lot, but my legs and bits are much better now … but it tickles awfully … I'll tell you all about it later…' She is rising from the settee in response to a signal from the guy in the suit '… when we are alone again and doing the other photographs … Proff.' Adams says we can do them tomorrow after lunch-break ... Just come to my classroom … like before?'

Jules replied with an unsure 'Thank you', and then follows her with his eyes as she walks towards the man. And when she reached him, she looks back for a moment with what Jules imagined is a slightly frightened or apprehensive look which reminded him of the existence of 'the secret thing' of which she shouldn't speak.

The colour photographs were taken using a Roliflex. It belonged to another student and there was some interference from one of the tutors which enforcing an uneasy silence. It was, Jules thought, a complete pain.

And then they were left to wait – amongst a stack of abandoned cinema equipment – while the colour film was processed by one of the photography students with the help of a technician. [24]

Jules found a perch on the low running board of a huge tracking dolly and his model stood close by next to a huge tripod. He had wanted her to sit next to him. It was her choice confiding and pre-empting her story by saying

'Thank-you Jules, but I'm still a little tender ... everywhere ... and although I know it means I'm getting better, the tickling is driving me quite mad ... I'd much rather stand ... Honest.'

A Disturbing Story

Jules is sitting only a few centimetres above floor level on the metal step of a tracking dolly; with his friend standing in front, her lower body pressed against a large diameter tubular camera mounting... the pleats of her short skirt stretch over her tummy ... only a few centimetres away from his up-turned face.

It is late afternoon and the room, which is somewhere on the fourteenth floor, is yielding without protest to natural darkness, but there is one distant and slender slash of brightness left in the evening sky.

Jules speaks first, purposely bypassing her earlier reference to tickling, but with its possible implications in mind he asks

'Tell me ... has your bike really got a puncture?' and to his temporary relief, she answers directly

' ... Yes it does ... and it's a real nuisance ... me not being able to use it.... It's the front one and I could mend it myself ... easily ... but ... I don't know if I told you ... while I'm doing what I'm doing, I'm having to live in this horrible hostel place ... and the women who are supposed to be caring for me are awful ... like prison warders ... really beastly and bossy ... I told them all I needed was a puncture outfit and a bucket of water, but they won't listen ... it's something to do with the smell of the rubber solution or something ... Honest ... how silly is that? Do you think I could do it at your flat?'

Jules agrees – it's something he can do in return for her being such a super model. And there's the hardware store nearby which is bound to have a repair kit -- and his flatmates shouldn't mind – all they would have to do is get the machine down the stairs or find a way round the back of the Mansions. They've had push-bikes of their own – Roger has one still, even though he's graduated, via a worn out and unbelievably heavy Mobylette, to a trendy Lambretta.

They might even help.

'Thank you that would be nice ...' she says thoughtfully, adding straight away and in a brighter voice, '... I would love to see where you live ... '

And with the ice sort-of broken, Jules dares ask about her accident – but without admitting that he had crashed a bike when he'd run out of brakes riding his older brother's machine and had steered into a hedge at high speed to prevent a more serious accident – and that, even though most of him and the heavy machine had penetrated deep into the dense Hawthorne before the rear swung around and pulled him out bouncing him several times on the road with Jules, bravely or stupidly, clinging onto the handlebars. His trousers had been virtually torn from him at knee level by contact with the rough road surface and his exposed skin filled with grit, but despite all this he'd limped away with just one large bruise on his leg from the leather saddle.

'Tell me ...' Jules is re-visualising the girl's injuries and comparing them with those he'd sustained '... but only if you would like to ... about your accident. If you were hurt like that, just coming off your bike, it must have been some crash'.

The girl answers him with a question

'How long will it be ... do you think ... before the film is ready?' she is making the tripod leg push deeper between her legs. He tries not to notice and says.

'I don't know really ...'

He is looking up at her face peeping over the turtle neck of her ribbed jumper and thinking what a great photo this so-close view would make – The shape of her torso perfectly defined, swaddled in those contours of ribbing – hugging her. And nearer to his eyes – his imaginary lens – her skirt – its box pleats rendered flat or full as they stretch over hips and tummy – what light and shade there is – And below the convex taught bow of her tummy there is a darker cleave from which a cold metal tube bursts out gleaming for a moment in a shaft of sunlight.

... I haven't done any colour processing, but I could guess at twenty minutes or so ... perhaps as much as half an hour ... Is it OK for you to wait that long? '.

She answers

'I'm in no rush to go home'

And he says, wondering if he has enough cash in his pocket to fulfil the idea

' ... We could go somewhere together...'

It is only an idea.

'I'm sorry I was away from school ... and for so long' she says, pre-occupied, '... and making you so terribly late with your project and everything ...'

'You mustn't be ... it wasn't your fault ... and it's giving everyone a chance to show what they can do ...by pulling all the stops out.... I think Prof. George must like us, or you, a whole lot.'

He is thinking '... who could not like, or love this girl – including Prof. George.'

She isn't listening – She is looking past Jules and is talking, as if to herself; or some invisible person standing behind him, or the increasing cloudy darkness outside of the windows.

' ... I couldn't help it ...' she is saying, almost apologetically, '... you see ... you're quite right... it was more than just an accident with my bike. ... Much more …'

She had been on her way home from College – riding her bicycle past a park – a car had moved alongside – far too close and trapped her and the machine against some metal railings – the left handlebar had caught and tipped her over into the road – her legs were tangled in the frame. but some men had come – she'd believed to help her – one even picked up her bike and risked being run over to rescue her bag from the evening rush-hour traffic – another had lifted her bodily and carefully over the railings into the arms of another who, in his turn, had carried her away from the smelly traffic and into the park where he laid her carefully on her riding cape which someone had spread on the ground. Her broken bicycle was laid nearby – she knew this because she heard its bell give a 'ping' as it touched the ground.

  It was a new bell and she'd hoped it wasn't scratched.

  The rest of her story she told to the dark space around her and behind Jules – there was no one else there - the lights were not switched on – the clouds had shut out the last vestige of usable daylight.

  She told the sky about the men – how still dazed from the accident, they had taken her and held supine and helpless – described every repeated intrusion into her which followed – the texture of each man's clothes and his hair – the peculiar smell of him and of his breath. And even though, she admitted she had sometimes drifted into welcome oblivion, each time she'd regained a little of her senses, she had known which of them it was for a second time.

And then an occasion had come – a break in her ordeal when she was conscious and her torn and tender body empty – a longed for moment she'd feared would never come. – a time when no hand was holding her so hard she feared the bone beneath it might break; or pressing so hard against her mouth that she could not breath. – But she had not dared believe it, or move an inch, for fear the men or any one of them might still be there.

But she could not lay still – her little body had shivered violently – from cold or dread of what horror might be to come – but still she had tried as hard as she might – until at last, believing she must be at last abandoned, she gave up the futile battle and rolled – slowly – carefully – painfully – onto her side and with numb fingers had drawn her clothes under her and curled into a tiny ball. And like this she had waited for oblivion to overtake her again – her only desire, she tells the darkness, being to feel a little less cold.

Someone had rescued her; she thought it might have been one of those same men, but one who had not taken such an active part in the assault, or one with a pricking conscience about leaving her in the dark and cold to die, for she had said in her story:-

'I'm sure they all did it at least once ... apart from the driver... I don't think the driver would have done it.'

She had surfaced the following day, to find herself in a warm hospital bed, but still so exhausted she could hardly move and so traumatised she had imagined, or dreamed, her attackers had been men she had seen at her home... card playing friends of her step – papa's.

She called that idea 'Silly imaginings!'

Jules had been horrified almost from the very start, listening at first with total disbelief, not wishing to accept that there could be a grain of truth in the girl's story – Believing that if it was true it would be impossible to tell – and as if to add to his disquiet, she had been, all the while and unashamedly, rubbing herself slowly against the leg of the tripod – but this, when he'd discarded the other 'crazy' possibility, only added to his growing belief in the truth of things – hadn't she said she tingled, or was it tickled, awfully – which he'd imagined was due to the bruises healing?

And soon he believed that all she said had really happened. – It was not a young woman's imaginings – a sexual fantasy – or a screenplay – or something she dared not write in her English class – It explained the bruising too – and everything and as he re-lived it with her, a steady flow of silent tears had begun to flow over his cheeks.

Several times he had willed her to cease her terrible narrative and let him, if she would allow him, to gather her to him and, with his cheek placed next to her tummy, let him use all the will-power he could muster to ease the hurt, but he'd been prevented, not just by the fear of harming her further by just being a man touching her, but by the physical presence of that bloody tube. There had been no option other than to let the girl continue until she had completed as much of her story as she wished to speak, or could speak of.

He had tried – to say, to ask, to utter or even formulate a word or phrase of comfort, but even if he had, he would have been rendered helpless by the silent screaming in his head and the lump in his throat which threatened to suffocate him. He was trapped – lost inside her story with a small lake of tears growing at his feet.

So it was, he convinced himself, an act of self-defence, when in his imagination, he made the growing puddle of tears a shimmering sunlit pool – the pool at the foot of 'his' waterfall in which he'd bathed naked that summer and in the two summers before. [25] And in this imagining he places her there with him – the sparkling cascade flowing gently over her shoulders – around her neck and between her small breasts. And from there over his forehead, eyes and cheeks, one of which he has placed touching her tight little stomach – His idea – that the soothing stream might collect his healing tears and flow on – over and around her mound – to form a barrier (of love) against the next horror she might speak of, or make an imagined soothing balm to heal her.

And as the screaming subsides, he is able to hear her again.

She is speaking of her last assailant – a heavy slob of few words – who'd failed to emulate his accomplices and invade her body a second time -- the man with the hard-haired army great-coat which reeked of stale tobacco, beer, fish and chips, urine and fusty damp leather. He had breath as foul as a drain too and had taken an age the first time – and had been really rough and hurt her inside. He had lost his temper and given up his second attempt in favour of showering her face with foul sputum and verbal abuse -- while punctuating each short string of insults with ill-directed kicks.

Jules hears this, even takes some of it in through the anaesthetic roar of falling water. And in his imagination he turns his head and places a gentle healing kiss at the site of each cruel blow, willing his magic waterfall, another flood of silent tears and his compassion to heal the harm.

And much later when she is speaking of her rescue and the stream of hurt not so intense, he takes her by the hand and leads her a little way downstream, past the deep, benign and forgiving pool in which he had once immersed himself to die – to the shade of 'his' ancient stunted oak, where they lay together (as he and Sukie had a few months before) to introduce her to his confidants: the sun, the air, the sky, the wind, the clouds; and of course the all-knowing old tree. And that done – when the birds and the rabbits come to see them, each with their tiny inquisitive and playful offspring – he introduces her to them – and they exchange 'hellos' while damselflies dance their dance of love and encircled them with their healing magic.

These are imaginings. She has never been here – he has taken/borrowed a memory of a time with Sukie and replayed it with Wendy in her place to save him from feeling all of her pain. But then her narrative stops and a silence envelopes them – the sound of the stream is banished into memory to allow a harmony to fill the room and Angels to pass over and between them and the mass of film and photographic equipment which surrounds them.

Wendy breaks the silence and frightens Jules who fears his ordeal is not over

'I woke up in a bed with curtains all around it. It took me a while to realise it was a hospital – and there were nurses talking in whispers at the other side – I think they were talking about me – saying what a shame it was ... that such a pretty girl should have lost her virginity ... '

Jules didn't answer – it was the lump in his throat, even if he'd been able to think of a single helpful word to say, but he knows the statement is not true – not in a literal sense, anyway, – but before he can speak she continues,

' ... It was really nice them saying I was pretty, but will anyone want to marry me now? ... I would have to tell him ... my boyfriend ... wouldn't I? ... Because he'd know the first time we did it together...? '

Jules was thinking hard for something useful to say and believing the favourite story – about losing it while horse riding – would be of no use, he latches onto her using the 'lost' word and, to his surprise, he finds his voice

'But you didn't lose... it was stolen from you … and cruelly ... it was not your fault ... and your husband-to-be will understand.'

The girl takes a moment before replying and then asks Jules the question he fears she might ask. She is speaking hesitantly

'Has your other girlfriend … I mean … do you know … does she … is she ... your Sukie … still a virgin?'

It is a question Jules has no wish to answer – instead he recalls, unwillingly, a time when he'd tried to kill a man for bragging that he'd enticed Sukie and her close friends to an all night party – and, after plying her with alcohol laced with Librium, had slept with her. And the next day – his dearest friend – his love – had told him how boring the party had been – and that the best part had been the morning after when she'd walked in the garden. But she'd asked Jules if it was possible the man could have done it while she was sleeping and Jules, thankful that his 'love' was still alive and as innocent as always lied to her. [26]

What good would it have done for her to know of his fears? [27]

And now, avoiding answering his questioner he says

'We haven't done it and gone all the way... we haven't ever needed to ...'

Then he tells her of his fears – about the man 'Stanton'

' ... She's seeing another guy while I'm away ... I hope and trust just for company. But he's a charismatic fellow who looks ... for the entire world ... like one of those handsome baddies in Wild West films... You know the ones ... tall with long hair sometimes pulled back into a ponytail ... and he wears a long riding coat and boots ... and this is in the City.'

She interrupts him

'... and you think he might seduce her and she might 'sleep' with him?'

Her words are so 'matter of fact' they allow for the vulnerable Sukie to have given herself to Stanton and the two magical girls are as one.

'Yes, but ...

He is imagining the unknowing Sukie dancing naked to the Robin's joyous song, making the silence of Angels return.

'You really adore her, don't you?

Jules is still coming to terms with this new perspective and doesn't reply – Wendy continues

'...There are people I know ... who owe me. I could ask them to make him go away.'

Jules thinks it a strange thing for her to say and is about to ask how it might be done, when there is a momentary flash of light from a doorway and a technician appears waving a sheet of photographic paper as if it is a trophy – It is a sheet of contact prints – and the man's American drawl declares the negatives are O.K.

It is, of course, good news, but the two have no excuse now – to stay in the darkness and share more of their private worlds. –.they must return to the real one and their respective class-rooms.

And when they stand together, waiting for a lift in the hard artificial light, they don't, or dare not look at each other. It is for fear of something they cannot define, but they can feel the reassuring presence of an Angel, so it matters not.

And when the lift arrives and the automatic doors open to invite them in, they do so without a word. But when the doors have closed and the metal box begins its drop through thirteen floors – Wendy lets out a gasp of breath – and Jules dares to hold her – fearing that her legs, if they are as weak as his, might give way beneath them when their plunge is eventually checked.

And when the lift does eventually stop and ten seconds have passed – and the bell has rung – and the doors have opened – they are almost on their knees – frozen in time, without a wish between them to find the energy to stand free of each other or to step out into the outside world. But when they do, and they say goodnight on the steps of the college, it is as though they have surfaced from an exhausting dream. [28]

The next day a negative is selected from the contact sheet and a colour print made by one of the technicians. It is retouched by Jules with much instruction and a lot of hands on help from a tutor who, he believes should be in front of cameras and not behind them. However despite that minor distraction the project is completed and submitted for selection.

In the meanwhile Wendy is introduced to Jules's flatmates, who both feel they already know her, due to her pretty face turning-up in unexpected places, like in their bathroom when they wished for privacy, or on the French doors above the record player; each time insisting they were silent. And after her damaged bicycle is repaired Wendy asks Jules if she can stay – pleading with him and his friends, saying

'Please ... please ... please', and when the lack of a spare room or bed was tactfully pointed out she'd countered in her disarming and matter-of-fact way '... I will share with Jules ... I will be his London girlfriend ... his Sukie shouldn't mind ... after all she has her other when Jules is here in London'.

The idea had been very flattering to Jules, but put 'on hold'. So why is she here now?

Waking into a Dream

Jules is emerging from sleep and straining to compose, in half consciousness, a suitable 'rant' with which to confront the landlord's agent. The subject of such a rant ... the faulty guttering which is creating a cascade of water to wake him in the middle of the night.... But before he has put more than a few words together the sound is replaced by another; but not the relentless drip, drip torture which had always followed past cascades; this is an intriguing rustle, like the sound a garment might make if it was allowed to fall to the floor.

Then there is silence, and Jules is on the point of dismissing that sound as someone being very quiet as they left the building, or a sound from the room above, or just his imagination, when there is another sound and this is the opposite of mere noise; a delicate sound decipherable in his sleepy imagination as the tinkle of a multitude of tiny water droplets falling into a quiet pool.

And in that dreamy moment he remembers he has not spent the last few hours alone; and listens intently for the next sound, and then the next. And as he does he creates in his mind a sequence of images – a film-maker's storyboard – in which the girl Wendy is the key image. [29]

The layout of this small space is almost identical to the one in which he has shared so much with Sukie, with the washbasin at the foot of the bed and to the left, but here, instead of it being against a blank wall it is under the window and in his first frame he places the girl standing there with her back to him and his borrowed pyjama top discarded on the bed cover behind her.

And in the next sketch she is rinsing herself with the hard cold water; it is flowing through her fingers, over her slender arms and falling from them to make that enchanting sound.

And in the next - evidenced by the faint crunching of his hand towel, she is drying herself; and after a short while returning it to its horse to hang there limp and abandoned.

And when the bedclothes tighten over his feet, he waits with his creativity hanging in the air – poised like a raised pencil – impatient for the sounds which, he hopes, will allow a long delightful sequence in which she will choose items from the chair and cover herself. But no helpful sound comes. All he can hear through the delicate silence is the ticking of his wrist watch; its fine Swiss movement urging time to pass; and the sound of far distant voices emanating from an equally distant radio. And overlaying these, the sound of a heart beat which could be his – or that of the girl – he's not quite sure which.

Imaginings

Bereft of any clue, but impatient, he creates in his imagination a single frame in which his subject is sitting quietly in front of the wardrobes mirror in contemplation; It is a back view borrowed from a life drawing he'd made almost two years ago of Linda, one of those many art school models, but with Wendy's hair. And to the right of this, he draws another to serve as her reflection. It is an image which takes no effort to make, and, as it had done so many times, it carries him into a perfect charming recollection.

Sukie is standing in the doorway of his room on her way to the kitchen to make coffee – her attitude uncharacteristically triumphant; her body as naked and as perfect as Donatello's sculpture of David, which had … in case his flatmates returned… made him insist she covered herself 'just a little' and forgetting he too was naked – he reached over to pass to her his very best shirt, after which she had suddenly left in a flood of giggling. [30] It was to become, out of all their many intimate times together, their most perfect encounter.

Sukie returned with the coffee and Jules, having suspected the cause of her giggles and covered himself, and asked 'Did it frighten you?' and Sukie replied, to his delight and punctuated by more barely suppressing giggles.

'Of course not... I am so sorry ... It was it sticking out ... it looked so funny ... and then ... when you wriggled back on the bed and it bouncing about like it did ... it was ... I thought ...' She is holding back more irresistible giggles, ' ... as if he was waving at me ... I just burst ... I couldn't help myself ...'

She is placing the coffee cups carefully on the floor now, to kneel on the edge of the mattress, – she has a cup in each hand which makes the movement as elegant as a curtsy – and when the cups are safe she continues, apologetically

'... I didn't mean to laugh at him...'

She has placed a hand at each side of his face now, so she might kiss him. It is a long caress of a kiss which says to Jules, 'Dearest sticky-out little Jules who takes me to heaven ... I love you'. And when Jules comes back to earth he tells her

'Well, I'm glad that ... I ... It ...didn't ... but you see he does that naturally when I admire your pretty body and think of you in that special way ... or you kiss me like that ... I can't stop him ... it's his way of showing he loves you and wants to push into you. ... You must know that ... '

'... to make me pregnant by him and have his children?'

'Yes ... didn't you do it in Biology, or your mum tell you?'

'No... not really ... she didn't even warn me about my period starting ... I was terrified, well not terrified, more worried really when I started bleeding the first time ... I thought I just had tummy ache ... I was at school when it came, but the teacher ... it was in domestic science class ... She was really nice ... and she had some spare towel things and I went home with a friend and a note to give to my mum.'

'That must have been awful for you'

'It was more ...well ... sort of embarrassing'

Jules doesn't know when girls are supposed to start with their periods, and asks, expecting her to say thirteen or something like that.

'How old were you then'

'Eleven and a half or nearly twelve ... I think I would be twelve and a half when they got going properly... if they ever have, because, as you know they're still not all that predictable'

Jules changes the subject.

'We had Amoeba's and those Hydra some- things?'

'Yes ... was that it? In Biology' Sukie exclaimed. 'Were we supposed to get making babies from that?'

'Sort of ... That's what we did at school. Cell division and stuff ... not even birds and Bees ... I'd been really looking forward to them.'

Jules thinks of all they have done so naturally together, and in a moment imagines an unwished for future in which he is separated from his Angel and in the arms of another; a man she might trust as completely as she trusts him, and continues speaking softly

'But seriously you really should know about making children. It's very important ... I found out a bit from my mum ... and my dad ... and books we have at home... proper Encyclopaedias with diagrams.'

Jules is changing places with her now – all the time being careful to keep some of the bedcover covering him – and she seems to know his intentions and moves to face him and to expose her tummy.

And, with the two in juxtaposition he shows her where he believes her eggs are stored, saying softly 'just there', and where the tubes are, through which an egg might move each month – more like one every twenty days in his friends case – his fingertip caressing the taught and perfect flesh that covers them – his touch moving first from the right and then from the left.

'And here ...' he whispers, allowing his finger to flow in a small circle on the centre of her tummy ... it ... your tiny egg ... waits in a special magical chamber ... but it waits only a few days ... and if it isn't fertilised in that time ... your body makes another perfect, new and magical place, to receive another equally impatient egg.'

'...and for me to have our baby?'

Her words conjure an impossible future … A fantasy.

'Well ... for that to happen ...' he continues, looking into her eyes for clues for words to use '... well ... what you call my funny sticking out bit must push into you ... just here.'

He allows the back of his index finger to touch and rest tenderly across folds so soft they might invite a kiss – A kiss he dare not place for fear the slightest breath might cause them open and reveal the forbidden paradise he knows is hidden there. And as if to re-enforce that idea a gentle bolt of energy passes between them – like it does between their lips when they exchange their silent '*Could I be in love with you?*' and he wonders if it, the electricity, might be the power of Genesis.

And when he looks up into her Angel's eyes they are filling with questions and those tiny sparkling tears which, by means unknown to him, control his every action. And now they ask what it might be like and he answers;

speaking words without knowing, but with imagination.

' ... It will be really beautiful ... for both of us ... I promise.'

Their coffees are cold now; and long since forgotten, and they lay side by side to rest in silence and he imagines she moves astride him and, when settled there, whispers 'I want us to' – and the sensations, in the extended fantastical dream which follow – surpass any he might have conjured before when alone in the quiet of night or morning.

And when all is spent he and his lover let time stand still. [31]

A Distraction

'Juuuules'

Jules surfaces a little, but keeps his eyes softly closed so he might imagine for a few more moments that his Sukie is really there with him and the tangible warmth he can feel on his face is hers.

'Time to wake-up ... I think'

It is not Sukie's voice. He is no longer dreaming. He knows it is Wendy.

' ... Is it really ... I was having the most wonderful dream *of Sukie.*'

He does not speak her name.

'I know' her words are whispered compassionately – as if she is as sorry as he is that his dream has ended. – Then she adds, after a reflective pause

'Did you see her at half term...?'

It is as though, like Sukie, she has the power to read his thoughts – but it is a welcome question too – one with an answer he can give with ease to divert his mind away from an impossible idea which has crept in.

'Yes … and she was as beautiful as ever.'

'And her handsome baddy ...' she asks, in a cautious inquisitive tone, 'I can imagine you meeting him and it being like in a 'Western', with you and him exchanging deadly looks across the street?'

Jules does not answer; he is remembering Sukie asking him if her virginity could have been stolen while she was asleep -- his unconvincing answer -- and what might, in the few magical minutes, have happened to him, especially as Wendy is astride him – like Sukie in his dream.

Wendy continues.

' ... You said he was a big man with the look of a handsome and dangerous baddy … didn't you? I can see you both now … you looking smart in your black cords and wearing your best black Stetson and him; as large as a horse with long tangled hair and wearing a long overcoat'

Jules had forgotten he'd told her about his Stetson; and preferring to recall a known past than confront – even obliquely – the barely believable and surreal present, so he answers

'Yes … he was there ... but not across the street. He was waiting for her in the doorway and almost blocking anyone else's view of the windows, but I didn't realise it was him until much later. I was so impatient to see her I pushed straight past him.'

Wendy is snuggling her knees against him and the bed springs squeak in pretended protest,

'It was a little like that ... but not quite ...' Jules takes a breath '...for a start, I wasn't wearing my Stetson.'

'Oh Jules ... your poor Sukie ... she must have been mortified ... with both of you there at the same time.'

Jules reflects for a moment or two, then agrees,

'It was a real mess. I've spent hours since reflecting on how it could have worked out differently, but ...'

'Have you fallen out then? '

'...with Sukie? No... I never could ... what-ever ... Anyway I don't believe she realised that I suspected it was him.'

'And you didn't say?'

'No I thought it best to keep quiet and allow her separate lives ... her two worlds to remain separate.'

'And the Baddy ... did he know who you were?'

'He may have... you see we had met and talked on a few occasions ... and he isn't a baddy actually.' Jules didn't 'snap'; he knows she used the term innocently, but still explains, just in case; 'I think he's an OK sort of guy really ... Yes he's a little intimidating when you first meet him ... It's his large frame and long unkempt hair that does it, unless he's pulled it into a pony tail. And, of course, there's his rugged good looks'.

'Gosh'

'Yes, he's handsome in that dangerous way that you young women seem to find so attractive … you know what I mean … and in conversation and close up his eyes can be really gentle, suggesting there is something of the vulnerable about him.'

Jules recollected a conversation between them in the coffee bar and continues,

'He once told me that he was an orphan … that his parents had been killed in an dreadful house fire … It was an awful thing to happen, but still ... a man of twenty nine or thirty describing himself as an orphan seemed a little strange to me.'

Jules stops abruptly, fearful that in his ignorance of her life, he might have 'put his foot in it' and said something out of turn which might upset her.

She cut across him in a soft voice

'It's all right', she says. (She has moved even closer to his side and although he can't see any detail of her his imagination tells him she is tantalizingly lovely)

'I think you should put some clothes on ...' (He is assuming a mock parental tone to combat other less defendable feelings) '... before you catch your death of cold…'

It was not a good idea, because she moves back astride him and pushes her tummy forward, saying insistently

I really don't feel the cold at all ... look ... I bet you can't see a single goose bump ... anywhere.'

There isn't, even though the temperature of the room is no less freezing than it was those few hours before when he stood beside the bed and shivered with cold, but he insists, saying

'...because it's ... not seemly for a girl ... when she is with a man ... even if she has ... they have ...'

Jules stops, realising what he was about to say – His dream of Sukie; her quiet out of character boldness; her incredible soft and welcoming warmth; her gentleness followed by his effortless coming – all of this had not been a developed script of a recurring dream – it just might have been real. And he finishes his sentence carefully, almost questioning

'... even if they have made a kind of love together.'

A fear is ploughing through him now – thoughts of a child – a future in ruins.

Wendy sees it and says quickly.

'Jules ... you were dreaming of Sukie and whispering her name ... and I wanted it with you ... and to be pregnant by you ... but you mustn't worry ... I won't tell anyone who it was ... you see I want your baby inside me and have that something beautiful ... to love and hold and everything while I am hidden away in the back of beyond ... I wanted it more than anything else in the whole world ... please forgive me'

For Jules this was a dream to share with Sukie – a perfect thing – the result of giving way to a pure unquestioning love, but still he wants to take the girl Wendy under the sheets and hold her still and warm and safe in his arms – and perhaps kiss her, but the momentary chance is lost – the gentle tension broken by the sound of a time signal from that distant, intrusive, radio.

'I will get dressed ...' she says, suddenly as if that proclamation might make him feel better, adding '... but only if you really want me to ... but please finish telling me about you and Stanton ... surely you don't really feel sorry for him ... He is after your beloved Sukie'.

Jules is imagining his Sukie and Wendy as one beautiful person and wants to say

'No ... I don't want you to get dressed – ever – I want time to stand still to give my world, my heart; my body all the time it might take for it to split into two so that I might live with and love you both'

But he knows that wish can't be – the supernatural can only go so far – so instead, he continues his story, but with a different mind-set to the one he might have started with.

'Yea ... But let the best man win ... fair contest ... and all that ...'

'What was unfair?' she asks,

'Well it was one of her friends at her place of work ... the Jewellers shop ...'
Wendy has moved to the foot of the bed, where – with her little bottom in the air – she is separating her clothes from those of his and simultaneously, creating views so enchanting he attempts to memorise every one of them – the play of dim light over her small form – the soft

muted colours of her flesh – the way her hair moves across and hides her face then parts momentarily to reveal the profile of her face against the window. [32]

She is a moving living 'life' sculpture and truly captivating – an image of a girl to fall in love with – and if he'd been a fine artist and had enough time with her, he might replicate her form in some material to do justice to her, (But is as yet un-invented) And then he remembers his promise of fidelity to Sukie and puts the possibility of loving another aside and returns to his story.

'Anthony spoke seriously out of his turn to Stanton. I was in the basement of the jewellers in a cafe area where, a little earlier, I had told Sukie, Anthony, and a couple of the others, about my Shhhhhh project – and you being my model – and I stupidly said something about London gangs and stuff

Sukie was in the space behind the windows, removing diamond rings from one of the window displays – so they could be stored away in the strong room – it was her special task in the half hour before closing.

And all was normal and under control – as if all was run by clockwork, but then there was a disturbance and I heard the staff talking excitedly.

Someone was outside – making a nuisance and the staff were discussing how they might move him on – I could hear quite clearly because the ventilators for the basement are under the windows.'

'Do you think it was him?'

'Yes. I do now, but I didn't then ... I even offered to help ... but Anthony ... he's the junior there ... He went.'

'Gosh'

'He was brave wasn't he? Anyway when all was done and he returned downstairs …triumphant, I asked him ... and he told me it was a guy who had been hanging around for weeks, leering at Sukie when she was in the windows and that Sukie had asked him, repeatedly, to go away and leave her alone, but he'd still kept turning up.

And curious, – and to some extent disbelieving, I asked him what the man looked like … I might even have begun to describe Stanton, but almost before I started Anton cut across me insisting that he was 'a short bloke' who moved on without a murmur after he'd been told Sukie's London boyfriend was there, and had gangland friends, so he'd better leave Sukie alone from now on or it would be the worse for him ...'

Wendy stops getting dressed and blurts

'Oh Jules, do you think he will get a gang together against you?'

She hesitates then and Jules wonders if she is thinking of the gang who had attacked her and he answers her quickly – just in case

'I don't think that... the gang thing …he has one already, made up of actors and the like, he's into music, books and theatre … Educated people like that aren't disposed to violence ... are they?'

Wendy laughs, which pleases him.

'... As I said, he seems to me to be a good man at heart and a gentle one. I'm not fearful of him at all, just angry that Sukie has been so deeply hurt... I do wish it had been different.'

'Jules, I just don't believe you're saying this ... It sounds as though you like him.'

'Well he has been there for her when I wasn't ... and when her parents were being ...' Jules corrected himself, for he knew that Sukie's father was still refusing to speak to her, ' ... are being really awful towards her and all because of me. And he ... Stanton, promised me if he was to win her... he would be kind and gentle and treat her right and respect and honour her ... and I promised him the same, if I should be the winner, so I believed she was safe with him.'

'You promised each other that?'

'Yes'

'So now you see how much of a mess Anton made.'

'He wasn't to know... He didn't know....'

It is an attempt to console Jules

'...You mustn't blame him.'

'I do wish that he'd just asked him to move over to the other side of the street or something to avoid any embarrassment to Sukie and left out the threat. Because when we left the shop he was there – still standing tall, but a little forlorn, at the far side of the street.'

'And you're poor Sukie?'

'That was what was so awful ... It broke my heart ... You see her friends surrounded us as we left the shop, but mostly they were around her; steering her away ... while talking far too loudly and enthusiastically about some fictitious party ... I bet just to try and distract Sukie from what was happening to her – and him ... But over the top of all that, and the noise of the city, I could feel his hurt ... and hear his silent screaming ...And his disbelief at what was happening to both him and his Sukie ... But more than anything I could feel his hurt ... his emptiness .... The same exact feelings I would have had if I had been in his place.... And I could tell that Sukie could feel it too, because I could see it in her eyes when she turned her head to look back at him – I felt all her confusion and her emptiness too.'

Wendy is still mostly undressed and still creating pictures.

Jules stops himself speaking aloud, realising that what he has describe could be, so easily, echoed later that morning, when he and Wendy part, and he finishes his story silently to himself ...

'Oh Wendy, Sukie's face was so full of bewilderment ... and a kind of sorrow ... her whole body seemed to say," I don't want this ... this something that is happening to me ... this enforced and unwished for sudden choosing" and I felt and shared with her an overwhelming emptiness'.

Then he speaks aloud

' ... I knew then that she loved him ... loves him ... most likely as much as she once loved me. And he had been there when she really needed someone when I was not. And I fear that now, should he stay away, she will love him for the rest of time, but perhaps worse than that ... not there and at her side to deter others.'

Jules's story was over and selfish Jules, the clot, had rambled on as a way of blotting out his intimacy with her – instead of celebrating it – and now he is embarrassed and once more lost for words. But he is rescued when she stands next to him and carefully wraps herself in her skirt. [33]

'I think the way you are about your Sukie is just so wonderful.'

And when she has recovered them and put on the black shoes and is fastening the straps she asks '...Does she know how lucky she is ... to have both of you?'

It was not really a question – and anyway Jules is lost to the moment – admiring and attempting to quantify the qualities which have allowed her to triumph over all that dreadful ugliness in her past.

'I'd love to make breakfast for you ... while you get dressed' – she is reaching for the door – 'Can I?'

She doesn't wait for a reply; instead he is presented with a cascade of more beautiful images – each and every-one perfectly framed in the paint chipped doorway – a faery dancing – flashing eyes – a cheeky smile that might be triumphant, topped with soft brown hair bouncing – flying – caressing her smiling face. And on his eye-line – a hemline – a pattern of box pleats spinning and lifting to reveal a pair of neat knees and pretty legs.

But before any of this can register all is suddenly wiped away by Roger appearing from nowhere – to collide with her and catapult his newly purchased bread, margarine and bacon down the stairs.

The injured milk carton remains firmly in his grasp.

Breakfast

Wendy is helping Roger recover the groceries and although their (too quiet to hear) conversation could be inconsequential, Jules imagines it isn't and in an instant his selfish wish to be alone and re-create the last few moments – or better still – to lie back and re-live his entire fantastic dream, is replaced by an overwhelming desire to be at her side.

And in a moment he is standing at the sink; welcoming every freezing splash onto his face and into his eyes; and drying his face while trying very hard to ignore the latent scent of her, and in record time he is dressed and downstairs.

He is still combing his dampened hair.

'Good morning Jules ... do you like Cornflakes ...?'

It is her voice and Jules is astonished – he'd expected an 'atmosphere' not domestic harmony bathed in the sounds and aroma of frying bacon and eggs – but he still manages to say, reply, as he looks around. [34]

'Yes I do thanks ...' then wishing to join in and become part of the idyll, he says – as if it is their very first meeting of the day –'... good morning Wendy' and turning to Rodge he adds, knowing he is redundant, '... anything you'd like me to do?'

He, Roger, is monopolising his beloved cooker; Wendy is busying herself laying the breakfast table and his taste in music ('Petite Fleur') is already emanating from their transistor radio -- there is nothing much of use he can do.

And then Roger takes his eyes from his precious eggs for just a moment and asks

'*Sleep* well Jules?'

There is an emphasis on the word 'sleep' which Jules can't help but read, and, looking at Wendy's smiling face for approval, he replies

'*Yes* Roger ... Very well' and Wendy's smile becomes a cheeky one – without a hint of a blush crossing her cheeks, and Jules – unsure if he had answered her earlier

'... Just coffee and Cereal will be perfect ... thanks', adding 'I'll do the Coffee'

The radio begins to sing 'Do you Love Me' by Brian Poole and the Tremeloes and as the title refrain repeats, and repeats, Jules cannot stop his eyes settling on her face. The light is bright now and he can see that the red in them he'd tried so hard to re-touch away on the photographs, is gone now and all of her small body is projecting a safe contentment. And with this observation he allows himself to imagine how she might have reacted, if he had made love with her the way he did with Sukie.

Would this lovely girl have kept her eyes as wide open to guide him? And with that thought and a recalled vision of Sukie in her heaven, he says 'silently' to this girl and the absent Sukie 'I love you ...' and fearful he might have said the words aloud, adds quickly

'... I'd love you to share with us ... you must ...will that be O K Rodge, if I re-stock the cupboard later?' [35]

Wendy cuts across Rodger's unspoken reply.

'.. I went shopping with Rodge' and Will' on Saturday and we bought some extra stuff ... It was great.'

Jules is 'out of it'; his head full of disbelief

It is eight O'clock, or thereabouts, on a Monday morning; he's been away from the maisonette since late, or was it mid, Friday afternoon, or was it a week before? – he can't remember that far back – and in that short interval his two friends have acquired a live-in 'kid sister' who's helped them do the weeks shopping – and stolen his bed – and tidied his room and his clothes – and this very morning, impersonated Sukie so perfectly, she could have, as easily as anything, sneaked his sperm. And now this same girl is calmly laying the breakfast table – as serene as serene can be – beautiful in her own special way – not glamorous or excessively pretty, but full of that special 'something' which, when he had encountered it, Ruskin had called 'Lovely.'

Jules is stunned and, when Roger beckons him over, he crosses the room without hesitation or question, like a school-boy on his way to a dressing-down from the head-teacher.

He is right about the lecture bit, but it is delivered in a whisper so that Wendy might not hear.

'Look Jules. I don't know what she's said to you, but she turned up here to see you on Friday afternoon; and even though we told her that you wouldn't be back until late last night, or early this morning, she stayed ... insisting that you said it would be OK. You know you could have asked us first.'

Jules can't remember making any such arrangement but still says 'Sorry Rodge' and then asks, suspecting what the answer might be,

'Has she been any bother?'

Wendy has slipping upstairs and out of earshot.

'Well... no...' Roger admits hesitantly, '... far from it... more of an asset really, but....' His eyes are looking up at the ceiling in the direction of Jules's room, '... there's something not quite right about her – for instance she told us she hadn't anywhere else to go. Now how can that be? Anyway, with her saying that we let her stay and we let her come with us on Saturday night ... and you wouldn't believe ... when we were getting ready, she was wandering about as happy as you like near-enough stark naked. We recon she's jail-bait ... do you know I stayed up until nearly three in the morning to warn you she was in your bed ...'

The pictures are easy for Jules to imagine and he can't help but feel just a little bit jealous of his two friends, but makes an excuse for being so late

'I'm sorry Rodge ... and thanks ... but it was god knows what time when I got back ... the train ...' but he doesn't get to finish his explanation before Rodger asks

'Anyway what is it with you and girls and bedrooms ... who do you think you are ... Peter Pan?'

Jules can see himself as a 'Peter' flying with his Sukie to another world – he's kind of done that – but can't help seeing his 'Wendy', not as the young girl in the story, but the proud 'Tiger Lily' who, when captured by the pirates and left to drown in the rising waters of the Lagoon, was too proud; or too dignified; or too something-else to struggle in vain, or scream for help which she knows will not come.

Rodger continues triumphantly, taking advantage of Jules's thoughtfulness

'...do you know that the teaching staff had a special meeting ... about you and Sukie and that you were within an inch of being thrown out ... it was a good thing they didn't see those photo's you took of Angelique ... and here you are in London ... and your at it again.

Did you think no one would notice the state of her ... Wendy ... after that last 'so called' photo-session?'

Jules wants to counter with something in retaliation, but he can't think of anything apart from his 'stealing' his 'Venus from Woodford' so his friend continues

'... Lez 'spotted' you and her in the lift afterwards ... she could hardly stand, but he put it crudely ... like he does ... But come on Jules ... admit it ... you didn't just taking photographs of her.' [36]

To try and explain about Wendy would have served no purpose other than to expose her confidences, but that unbelievable few hours alone in the company of Angelique was different – it was only proper that he put Roger right – even though his most enduring memory is a picture of her lying in his bed with her pretty head and bare shoulders peeping out from under the covers; and her hair; and those eyes; *Were they asking?* And in front of this vision and to the side, that neat pile of folded clothes topped, as if in triumph, by a soft white bra; A sight for sore eyes provided by a model innocent of everything other than being very pretty and far too trusting. [37]

And after this moment of reflection he says

'Look Rodge ... all we did was create some really super photographs ... there was truly nothing else. And when she saw the contact sheet she apologised and, of course, when she asked me, I gave her all the negatives.' [38]

'But you made and kept some prints ... I've seen them'

'Well yes ... that's true Rodge ... but, honest, she looked so 'fabulous'; and I only printed two ... or was it three? And about the other thing ...They didn't chuck me out,

If you remember I got the prize for the student most likely to be a success in industry instead.'

Roger returns to the subject of Wendy spending the night in Jules's bed.

'God help you, if Wendy's parents were ever to find out …'

Jules can't recall Wendy ever mentioning her parents and after a moment of reflection, in which he wonders where they might be, he says

'I don't think they're around. And you're making unwelcome assumptions again.'

'Well someone's around ... because everywhere we've gone this weekend we've been haunted by these blokes ... big blokes and this car and ....' [39]

Wendy is no longer upstairs and in response Rodger's next words have tailed away or become so soft Jules can't hear them. And in a moment she is standing at his side reminding him of coffee and breakfast, so nothing more is said. And then William, ducking his shock of fair hair under the doorway, explodes into the room, calling cheerfully

'...Morning everyone ...'

It takes all the tension away and Jules and Roger, as always, amazed at how Will' can do this – manoeuvre his long and lanky frame down the last few steps to turn airborne through the narrow and low opening without cracking his head; breaking an arm, or doing some other great damage – forget their differences and give a long synchronised low whistle of appreciation.

William wishes Wendy a special 'good morning' accompanied by a little bow, and it is obvious to Jules that her presence over the weekend hasn't bothered him one bit because he sits by her other side and engages her in low conversation. And, in a further moment or two, Roger arrives with his plate of food and turns the radio dial to receive the BBC light programme, which effectively suppresses all conversation into spasmodic comment, opinion and friendly argument prompted by news of home and world events.

The trio are impressed by the girls input, as she seems to have far more developed opinions than they had, especially on the subject of law and order.

But she had overheard some of Roger and Jules's earlier whisperings and in a longer moment of quiet she ventures to explain.

'... Roger ... and you dear William ... please don't worry ...' her eyes are moving between the two, '... I must leave today ...' She turns to look at Jules, '... even though I would really love to stay ... I just came to see Jules ... to tell him it was time for me to go away ... a very long way away ... and to say a special goodbye to him.

But you Roger ... and you William, I've loved being here ... living here and getting to know you and sharing with you and everything.'

She looks to William. 'Especially the posh concert ... Oh... Will .... Please ... you must tell Jules about the music ... I can't remember what it was called. The one when I cried'.

Jules sees the last few words slip almost silently from her lips; lips he cannot believe he has failed to kiss, when, looking back, there must have been so many opportunities.

'You cried?' Jules was looking into her eyes again, and then at William's who rescues her by blurting his answer as if speed reciting the programme notes.

'It was Haydn's Cello Concerto number two. In D.' he gasps, '... and it was played superbly. I think you would have liked it Jules....' He takes a breath '... You see although it was written in seventeen ninety something, it's been lost even to history until just a couple of years ago ... and there's a bit in the second movement ... where the soloist is invited to do his own thing.'

'And boy did he do his own thing.' Roger gives his friend a chance to catch his breath.

'Well, that is why you'd have loved it Jules... with your love of Jazz and all that. You see he ...the first Cellist guy took the theme to New Orleans ... Haydn's seventeenth century theme ... and played it in style ... well all the audience thought he'd freaked out ... the guy was like Stephan Grapelli on Mescaline ... And this was on the Cello and at The Royal Festival Hall.' The last words are spoken as though he is describing an act of sacrilege.

'I thought it was really Fab.' Wendy is rescuing William now.

'But you cried' asks Jules, persisting gently with his question and trying to catch her eyes again

'The Cello can do that ...' Will explains, cutting in once more '... and there are some seriously melancholy bits too ... really beautiful.'

'No Will ...' she says and then corrects herself, '... You see ... Yes I was listening to it ... and it was very moving ... beautiful ... like the music on Sunday morning that seemed to float into Jules's room from nowhere. But it was not just that ...'

She looks to Jules and whispers

'... you see ... sitting there quietly, I began to think of you and me ... me saying things ... and you making me feel pretty again ... when I'd come to believe I couldn't ever again ... not even in my wildest dreams...'

Rodger and William, unable or unwilling to hear, take up their own conversation and Wendy turns so she and Jules are eye to eye; she taken his hands in hers

'I was so horrid to you ... telling you all those things ... and you were so good ... listening quietly to my silly stories ... and soothing me with your warm tears and surrounding me with all those pretty blue butterflies.'

The room falls so silent her last few words are easy for all to hear and create some wonder across and around the table, not least in Jules, because he's sure he had never told her about his imagining them beneath his waterfall; or about the clouds of Dragonflies; or them laying together under the ancient oak ... but there is no time for speculation because she has turned her attentions to Roger, who has just dispatched the last of his 'grand dejeuner.

She speaks apologetically,

'Oh ... and you Roger ... I do wish that I'd had a real mini skirt to wear for the 'Marquee' ... anything other than my boring old school thing.' [40]

No one is going to agree that any skirt, when dancing around her, could be boring and Rodger replies

'Perhaps there will be another time, but honest you looked pretty good to me ...' His tone is filled with understanding, even compassion, which surprises Jules. '... Honest you looked just great; like 'The Shrimp' in that advert ... but admittedly ... not so tall without the boots ... but your hitched up skirt made-up for that ... and some. Anyway you can always leave some proper weekend clothes here ... for another time.'

'There really can't be a next time'; she is speaking with a hint of sadness in her voice, '... you see ... as I said ... I must go away...' she turns to Jules, still speaking very softly, 'I should have gone on Friday ... but I came here instead ... I fixed it with my man in the dark suite ... that I could stay with a special friend ... He gave me the money for the food and stuff ...'

The men look at each other in silence. Then she adds with a grin

'I wish now I'd thought to ask him for a pair of white leather boots.'

The confused young men have nothing to say; perhaps they are imagining their friend in those boots, or trying to remember seeing a man in a dark suit. And Angels fly around and between them creating a silence which allows the radio to intrude. It is a man's voice speaking in that authoritarian way which is obligatory for announcers working for the BBC.

'... and the time is just a-quarter to nine',

There is a split second before the three men spring to their feet – and chairs fly through the air – air which is filled in an instant with muted expletives which refer to the stupidity of the word 'just' being so casually associated with 'a-quarter to nine'. And the men gulp down mouthfuls of coffee and crash into each other. And dump dishes in the sink, stopping only briefly to throw precious food into the waste bin beneath it.

Jules looks at his watch – his Father's – which keeps almost perfect time and which he'd remembered to alter by an hour, just yesterday; It 'says' just after ten past eight; He puts it to his ear; The Swiss mechanism which, a short time earlier, he'd wished might distort time is working perfectly. He puts his fingers to the winder. It 'takes' just two turns to prove it is fully wound so he stops rushing about and observes the chaos.

Wendy is behaving just as J M. Barrie's invention might have done, instructing Roger and William in a calm matronly way to please set-off for college this very moment, and to leave everything – all the washing up; and the tidying up; and the bed making – to her. Insisting that, if they did, they could easily 'make it' in fifteen minutes. But they must get a move on and, not to worry, she will drop the catch on her way out. All could be a last thank-you gift to them.

Jules is left to decide his own actions, but fills the immediate moments by replacing the chairs; clearing the last things from the table and shaking the tablecloth out of the French doors.

She is standing by the sink and Roger and William, obedient to her, are upstairs noisily assembling their stuff for college.

Jules goes to her side, wondering, and thinking

She has always been a bit 'scary'... that childlike trust she has; but brave too; But to say what she had at the breakfast table, she must have shared his private imagining – and seen herself standing naked and bleeding beneath his waterfall...his head against her tummy and the rest.

This is, or was, how she'd been able to 'be' Sukie earlier; She must be like her... magical in that way which is beyond nature, but still of nature ... a réciprocophité, if that might be the word for someone who can share thoughts with another without any effort or a single prompting word.

They do not speak; and in the 'loving' silence the disembodied voice in the radio returns to apologise for its previous mistake.

Jules shouts up the stairs

'Rodge; Will' ... Stop panicking ... It's only quarter past eight'

Jules's dad's watch was right, only two minutes fast, and with more muffled and less profound swearing, the confusion is put to one side and a kind of normality returns in which Jules is drying Wendy's meticulous washing-up.

'You know those little blue butterflies?' she asks, submerged the last plate in the sink and propelling Jules, unwittingly, into his valley with her and the dancing Dragonflies (Calopteryx splendens) not Butterflies. But this is no time to be a pedant so he picks a pretty blue butterfly he knows of to fit her mistake

'Yes ... I think they're called Holly Blues, but they won't know we call them that – and, of course, they'll have a scientific name, but I don't know what it is'.

She is withholding the last plate from Jules by holding it suspended in mid air between them,

' ... Holly ...' she says, as if far away in thought, '... I think that's a nice name'

Jules replies, imagines her lying next to him; warm and soft, if he dared to hold her to him, not a bit hard or prickly. But it sounds nice enough and he wonders if she is thinking of a new name for herself and answers.

'Yes... it's very nice, but I think it's a little bit prickly for you.' And she replies

' ... Perhaps' and the pair exchange smiles. And she relinquishes the plate and in that moment the imagined Dragonflies – or Butterflies, who had become Angels, set them free to collect their portfolios and their bags and to don their outdoor clothes.

Wendy only has her basket and her duffel coat, but still she is the last to leave, having gone back into the maisonette at least twice if not three times. And it is Jules who sets the catch and closes the door behind her for the very last time; and sees her transfer a secret kiss from the tip of her index finger to the faded number on the door; and hears her whisper 'Thank you.' [41]

And when outside Jules remembers he should let the heavy, old and sagging outer door shut on its own, and when all four are through to the street side he lets-go of the ornate bronze handle and it hesitates as always – then stutters and shudders against the floor to create a voice for the Mansions which sounds and then re-sounds in its stairways and landings. It says

'... Deeeeeearest Wendy – it's been aall my pleasure.'

And when it eventually slams shut it says and repeats '... all my pleasure; my pleasure, my pleasure' and Jules and Wendy wait politely for it to finish.

Uncle Pierre and Men with Guns

The wide pavement of Kennington Road is alive with people; some talking loudly with friends and eager to start their working day, while others walk alone with down turned blank faces – as if lost in thought, or in dread of the horrors their day might bring – all are moving North, towards Westminster Bridge or Lambeth North tube station.

Jules and Wendy, with the voice of the mansions still filling their senses, step out against the flow and collide and become entangled with '... uncle Pierre ...' their friendly ironmonger. But he doesn't mind – the three are laughing – and a wide beam of a smile is growing across his rounded face. And in an instant he has grasped Jules's hand and is pumping it enthusiastically in congratulation – and then – apologising for broken etiquette – he takes Wendy by both hands and kisses her three times on each side of her bewildered face – starting with the left.

He knows they will be happy together always – and they must have lots of children – He is looking tenderly at her flat tummy invisible beneath her duffel coat – He has known this from the first – And he must be invited to the wedding – and all the Christenings.

Then he is swept away and although lost to view in the crowd, he still insists his points at distance, but now it seems the children must all be girls.

It is an absurd idea. The man is mad – deranged. And the lovers, he imagines them to be are left speechless, not least because the dear old man, in his wisdom, has touched a nerve and voiced for them a latent crazy idea – an impossible dream.

In the real world and across the road from them, the grey Riley, from the very earlier morning, has been joined by a carelessly parked another, and the drivers are in conversation. The stockier one is stuffing something bulky inside his inside jacket pocket and both are looking towards Jules and Wendy, but as their eyes meet they turn to look North towards the Hercules, where, just visible to them and behind the twin telephone boxes, men in white coveralls and boots are unloading a plain white van and beyond them a uniformed police officer, wearing huge white gloves, is directing traffic towards the river and the Houses of Parliament while the robotic traffic lights ineffectually repeat their unchanging sequence.

And to the South, in Kennington road, Roger and William are almost out of sight, walking side by side against the flow. The subject of their conversation or even the odd word inaudible to others over the sound of traffic – but most likely a reflection on a weekend so different from the one they might have planned – they might even be discussing Jules breaking – yet again – the 'no girls' rule made when they'd first taken the lease on 'One A' – The rule Jules had insisted must allow for proper girlfriends, as opposed to casual ones, just in case Sukie found a way to visit him or came to stay. Sukie would always be special.

And now that rule has been broken and Jules's promise of unending fidelity to Sukie complicated by thoughts of a parallel one he might wish to give Wendy – one re-born by their Uncle Pierre's charming outburst – Wendy's impossible idea of him living two parallel lives.

So they walk in a submissive silence to the junction with Lambeth Road where they must wait for the lights to change so they might cross to the east side of Kennington Road.

One of the Rileys or one very similar, is standing at the lights and they cross in front of it and Jules, out of curiosity, looks inside. The leather case is still perched on the dashboard, but in daylight it seems different – a second look is prohibited by the eyes of the occupants.

In Lambeth Palace Road he shows Wendy the blue plaque on William Bligh's house and, for something amusing to say, suggests there might be a plaque for them one day – perhaps to the right hand side of the Mansion's door – between it and the hair dressers – people might stop to read it and expect the citation to say something really important – historical stuff – and be surprised when it just reads 'Wendy slept here with Jules in 1963'.

They laugh and Wendy asks if he and Sukie would have lots of children – like the 'lovely Mister Pierre' had suggested – and did he know that they, the Bligh's, had had five girls – '... he was Cook's Navigator on the Resolution you know ...'

Jules wonders how William Bligh had found the time when he was at sea so much. And recalls what little he knows of the mutiny story and how dignified and calm Bligh had been during the mutiny – like Wendy, when she'd related her story to him – a special quality which would be wasted '... in the back of beyond'.

And not for the first time he has doubts of the truth of it all and sees images of her 'rape' in his head – each one cascading onto and over its predecessor – like developing photo prints – and when he dares to let himself 'see' them he sees what he always sees – injuries that are real enough – four, five, six and another higher on the left inner thigh. And on the right – another, which makes seven – and another – eight – and another –

He is pulled into the road. It stops the images and in the next moment he and she are weaving in and around standing traffic towards the park. And when safe at the other side and on the pavement Jules, in need of a stream of pretty images as an antidote imagines a future life for Wendy and says

Imagined Futures

'You know ... if you could only stay in London you could be on the T.V. Perhaps presenting the news ... your voice is so clear ... and you've got the looks ... People ... blokes anyway ... would tune-in in their tens of thousands just to look at you'.

He'd nearly said 'Gauped'.

She doesn't blush – instead she joins in his fantasy using a voice not her own, but a stereotype of those she has heard on the Television or radio

'This is the six O'clock news ...' she says, '... and this is Wendy Renard reading it.'

He corrects her – using his own version of the announcers rather upper-crust and pompous style

'... The *beautiful* Wendy Renard reading it'

They both know that 'play acting' an impossible future is their only refuge.

'If only ...' she says, thoughtfully ... touching his hand and equalising their electricity '... but you would have to be my cameraman ... every night of the week.'

She is looking at Jules who is imagining driving a half ton television cameras – it isn't for him, even if they do float on air – and he lets her continue

'... you are so amazing with a camera and soon it's all going to be in colour – The thing ... don't you think.'

Jules agrees.

She is holding his hand strongly now, or he is holding hers – he is not sure which. And their grip tightens with excitement when two foxes appear. They are crossing the road and when they reach the pavement they stop; blocking their way forward.

There is a haunted, almost desperate look on each narrow face, which prompts Jules to crouch down and speak gently to them; thanking them for coming to see them and suggesting to the dog fox that he should be more careful of the traffic – after which they slink away – first one and then the other through a tiny gap in the huge gates, but not before Jules has registered another 'freeze-frame' of Wendy crouched down and talking to the vixen.

There is a notice above the gap. It lists the opening times – On Mondays, during the winter months, it is 10.30 am to 4.30 pm.

Jules instinctively looks at his watch. It is fifteen minutes to nine – and two - hundred miles away his Sukie will be arriving at her place of work – he can see her, in his imagination – smartly dressed and as simply beautiful as ever behind the false glamour of make-up – She is crossing the broad street as safely as he might wish – holding hands with Stanton who is challenging the traffic – daring it to come too close. It doesn't.

Opposite the Museum a Harrods electric delivery van creates a historic picture against the elegant buildings. – A black cab and two busses crawl past it – nose to tail – to be replaced by several private cars. And when the busses move on towards the junction, Jules can see the green van has stopped. And behind it – entrapped by a seeming endless stream of traffic – is the grey Riley saloon.

Jules takes Wendy's hand – wishing a gap in the traffic so the men might see – '... *they can think what they like.*' and they walk on in the company of their Angels.

Ahead of them Roger and William are striding out and have disappeared from view behind the shrubs and trees which, together with an iron fence, mark the north-east corner of the still frost covered park.

There is a gate into the park there on the corner and when they reach it – its pad-lock, thwarts a belated idea to be away from the traffic and alone together for a few minutes and out of anyone's sight. And in the next minute they see their destination, its tower the tallest in view, and made of glass, plastic, steel and concrete – but this morning it thinks it is made of imagination – its silver blue panels in competition with the glass of the windows in their quest to reflect the greatest amount of the first fragile light of Monday.

And Jules looks up and counts downward from the top to see if he can identify the floor and the window behind which he and Wendy had shared so much, but he can't, and denied that contact with the real he releases his gentle pressure on her hand; and in return she releases hers on his

Their unspoken idea – their unknowing idea – to begin to part and make the inevitable rift less sudden – but now they are separate the power holding them in this fleeting diversion from 'real life', is even stronger and forbidding them to touch again for fear it might ground the magnetism and spoil the exquisite tension – or complete a circuit and unleash who knows what.
[43]

And now their Angels tease them, showing them more imaginary plaques to commemorate unspoken and preposterous ideas. One is beneath a street nameplate on their right. It reads

'Holly ... who was Wendy, together with Jules Renard made a mad dash down this street towards 'West Square' on 4th November 1963. ... and they had no idea why.'

And in a moment it changes and reads

'... to escape the unwished for inevitable and be together always, or for just a little bit longer – an hour – a morning – a day – anything.'

And in their heads they imagine they might catch hold of one another and with that unspoken thought the lettering on the plaque changes again

'... to find somewhere to make love.'

Jules looks around; A little way behind them, mixed in with a gaggle of students, are two men in long coats. They are walking purposefully in their direction... And to his left down what might be an escape route towards 'West Square' there is another man, identically dressed, immerging from the mist.

And to his right, St. Georges Road is denied them by two double-decker busses, parked nose to tail and emptying passengers.

There is nowhere for them to go, but forward towards the college where they might hide for a few minutes among their fellow students who, instead of entering the building, are standing about in small groups, which as more and more students arrive, threatens to form a solid mass bounded on one side by the towering college buildings and on the other by the roundabout and roadside railings – a fortification of students.

It is in the middle of this wall that they come to a final stop – two students undistinguishable from a thousand others;

Some are talking; speculating as to why they are standing out in the cold.

One voice asks -

' ... Do you thing think there's been a break in ... what would they take?'

Another -

'... I've heard the place is chock-full of Police ... some with dogs ... and that more are coming'

' ... Angie says some have guns.'

And another who has pushed through the throng -

'... There's a fire tender round the back ...'

Another - excitedly

'... That makes three counting the one with the long ladder'

Jules reassures Wendy

'It must be a fire drill or something, or perhaps a real fire, perhaps a spontaneous one in a dumpster ... There are several around the back ... in the space between the tower block and the workshop building ... all would be full of rags soaked with stuff that can burst into flames ... just for the fun of it.

They have caught up with William who overhears and adds

' ... Or it's homeless people who have been burning stuff to stay alive.' [44]

Wendy has placed herself directly behind the lanky William and Jules behind her to protect her from the crush. And it is here, shielded from the milling throng, where she turns to face Jules, and speaking to his chest and with her head pressed lightly against it, she says

'You know it's time for me to go now?'

'Yes', Jules is looking down at her hair and then her upturned face.

'I don't know where I'm going ... they haven't told me ... and as you've guessed, I must have a new name and everything ... everything has to change ... and I must never come back ... or write to friends ... or do anything that might give me away.

They say it's the only way I will ever be safe from those men ... the men in jail ... or others they might send to kill me.'

'Sheesh ... have you upset someone that much?'

She places a finger against his lips, like she had done at his request for the photographs and ads

' ... And if I could hear that you loved me ... I will never ever forget it ... I promise ... because when I need someone and there is no-one ... I will hear you ... I don't think I will be able to bear it ... going away ... unless you say you do'.

Jules has never seen a proper tear form in her eyes before, but now he can – they are soft tears which he knows, if he were to kiss them, will taste of honey – and when he looks closer he sees the tears as reflections of those filling his own eyes. And when she moves her finger from his lips to let him speak, Jules feels that if he lets that idea into his heart it might break. But still, he does as she has asked and says – 'I love you ...' – believing in that moment that he is lying, but then finds himself adding silently – almost unwillingly ' ... *and I fear it will be for the rest of time. And still I haven't kissed you'*

And with his eyes blinded with tears he opens his arms to fold them around her – wishing to hold her for the first and last time in the gentlest of hugs – to imagine he can feel her warmth next to his warmth at least this once and perhaps revel in the joy of feeling her hair touch against his face – he might even feel the beating of her heart. But before his arms can close around her, a roar goes up from the crowd – and he looks away from his 'pretend' love, just for a moment, to see the doors of the college are opening.

A Bunch of Flowers

And he closes his arms to find she is as light and insubstantial as an idea – or a bouquet of flowers – flowers which have a fragrance of soap – his soap – the soap he brings from home and which she used this morning to wash before she ..., or was it after?

His arms are empty; instead there is something warm entered him under his ribs. At first it seems like a dagger, or a switch blade is pushing in there, but there is not a hint of pain or of a sharp edge cutting – only a feeling of warmth penetrating deeper and deeper into him – dissipating – dividing and re-dividing as it goes – each time releasing a tiny pulse of soothing energy. [45].

It is a feeling so enchanting he stands as still as he can, imagining it is her – her 'beauty' which is moving inside him; touching and exciting vital parts as it does. And he holds onto this fantasy until he is eventually dislodged, from what he imagines must be a magical spot – a portal to another world.

And when the crowd has passed he turns to find the place where they were standing is just a place; a paving slab inscribed with a reference to its manufacturer and the assertion, or is it a guarantee, that it is 'none slip'. He knows it is the right one, because although it is indistinguishable from thousands of identical neighbours, there is a small black shoe perched there which has a rounded toe and a raised heel and its strap-over fastening is broken.

At the lost property desk, the clerk in charge is a bit bossy and insists, impatient with Jules, that she can't find a record of a student named Wendy – The student index doesn't work that way – she must have a surname or know which year she is in; or the subject she is studying; or it will take forever. And in the meanwhile he must leave the shoe with her.

And, put-off in this way, Jules parts with the shoe, consoled by an idea that his Wendy will have no need for it now. She is living inside him – and in the next moment he begins to believe she'd always been there – that she hadn't ever been real – only a figment of his imagination, and the more he thinks this, the more likely it seems. And as he walks away from the desk he says to himself.

'That was it – for her to be so lovely and so brave and so affecting and so bold this morning – and the rest – she could only have been a figment of imagination.'

At the lifts 'Aspen' is standing, as always a head taller than everyone else, with the much shorter 'Jag' next to him, intimidating in his far too smart suit. And behind them are the calm and stately Hillary – and Edmund – and Robin and the vivacious Viveka, who has already discovered something to giggle about and is filling the air with her music.

Reality returns

It is Monday the fourth of November; a real day with real things happening and the first day of the winter term.

And when the working day is over and the evening meal made and consumed and associated chores are done – Jules sits quietly and writes a note to his beloved Sukie – and, to make sure she receives it, he will address the envelope to her place of work

> *'..... Dearest Sukie,*
> *Today ... after being stuck on the train in pitch dark for many hours somewhere in the wilds of Norfolk ... has been pretty uneventful ...*
> *But actually I didn't mind so much ... being stuck like that ... because it gave me lots of time to think of you ... and making love with you.*
> *I love you more than ever...*
> *Please take care...*
> *I will see you very soon and before too long with you for always.*

    Jules XXX

At Garelochhead Station

Jules's wakes now to find he is on a train. It is standing still. And through the carriage window he can see a rocky coastline bathed in warm light from a setting sun. In the foreground there is an oversize sign with equally large lettering – all in capitals and sans-serif. It declares the halt to be 'GARELOCHHEAD'. The sign spoils the composition.

    Inside the carriage his friend Paul, as in unmeasured time before, is sitting opposite him, alone, and the clutter of bags across the way has grown a little smaller.

'... Hi Paul ... so sorry for sleeping so long... ' and after a glance down the carriage,
'... What happened to the girl?'

His hope is that she's still on the train, or has just in this last minute stepped out onto the wooden platform, because if she has, he might see her again, not as the 'invisible' crew member he'd paid little or no attention to during the last two weeks, but as the person he might wish, or fear, she might be.

And while he waits for his friends answer, he pretends to suppress a sneeze, but is really covering his mouth and nose with his hands to breathe in the expelled air and quieten the thumping of his heart.

If she's on the platform he might call out to her – shout out something – anything which might make her turn her face toward him and allow him to see her – and she to see him – to speak an unspoken farewell – a simple wave might do – or a shout of 'God bless – please remember me to your sweet mum.' Or just eye contact – just for a second – anything.

Paul answers
'Jules, your sleeping was no matter. Don't worry about it ... two eight hour watches ... one after another ... and then staying above decks to witness our little ships home-coming ... I don't know how you did it ... you really needed those hours of shut-eye.

But you asked about the girl ... well I'm afraid she left the train a full hour or so ago ... at a place named Low something ... it was deep in the wilds ...'

Jules responds with a lie

'Oh ... its O.K. ... it's of no matter' and Paul speaks his own 'white' lie saying blandly

'... I believe you ...' then continues 'But, my dear Jules, you have missed out on such a treat ... I've been entertained for a full hour or more with a story you would not believe .... about her and her mother's past ... her bravery and her adventures as a government mole ... and it going wrong and becoming so dangerous she'd had to move to Scotland ... She referred to it as 'the back of beyond' ... to live the simple life and learn to shoot a pistol and a rifle. She'd become a crack-shot with both and taught her and her sister to shoot too ... at what she called 'stuff' and rabbits.

The old man's voice tails away, then, after a pause he says thoughtfully

'I'm sure if she'd learn to keep a secret she might emulate her mother ... But fancy calling herself 'Holly' ... surely it can't be her real name ... If she joined the service she'd have to change it ... it sounds so false ... a name borrowed from a novel'

Jules cannot resist his reply, but has to take a deep breath first

'Well Paul ... it takes a spy to know a spy.'

The carriage falls silent and in the dense quiet, amplified by iron wheels counting joints in the track, Jules repeats his earlier arithmetic – speaking silently to the girl in his heart;

'So today is your birthday ... baby Holly's birthday ... add three months ... take away a year ... it fits perfectly, but how about the decades between ... there are three not two ... How could you say you are only twenty-one years old and look it ... you should be thirty-one.

Paul interrupts his musing, as though he could overhear Jules's rustic mathematics, with his own thoughts, saying

'In the services we were made to believe there is no such thing as co-incidence – but I'm not so sure of the truth of that now – You see you're right about me having worked for the government, but it was not a bit dangerous ... there was no James Bond action for me ... I was far too old for that ... even back then. My main work was just to keep my eyes and ears open and pass anything interesting on to my old skipper ... he'd found an easy desk in Military Intelligence ... it was just bits of this and that ... mostly gossip I picked up on my expeditions to China and India when I was out there buying Tea.

I would be about your age then ... late forties or Fifty-ish?

'Good guess Paul'

'They ... the home desk ... were short handed for some surveillance duties ... and, being at a loose end, I did it ... It was for just one week ... Our focus was a young woman who'd infiltrated one of the London Gangs ... or had been unfortunate enough to be born into one ...or something of that kind ... who had turned informant ... a mole.

It shouldn't have been ours really, but we were investigating the Metropolitan Police at the time and there was some cross-over of interest ... so it was tasked to us to keep an eye on her and keep her safe for a few days until she could be moved away to safety.

'An easy- enough job then?'

'My partner would have said, "As easy as eating eel pie", but thinking back to then, someone pretty high-up in government must have really cared for her to allocate so much man-power ... There was at least two of us observing her twenty-four hours a day ... and we worked eight hours on then eight hours off ... not the eight on and sixteen off 'watches' like on our little ship. I remember it did nothing for my internal clock, or my nerves, when we were told to carry firearms just in case our target's one-time friends showed up.'

Jules asks – thinking of an impossible three-way co-incidence

'Just when was this Paul?'

'It would be in the nineteen-sixties ... sixty-three perhaps ... Yes, that would be it ... the autumn of sixty three and the beginning of that dreadfully cold winter. But we had an easy enough time ... we even went to a Sunday afternoon concert at the Festival Hall '

The words re-conjure Jules's time in London – those concerts – that one night and breakfast shared with Wendy – And the grey Riley saloon parked in the misty shadow outside the Mansions in the early hours of that Monday, and says

'I was in London that year ... and went to some of those concerts ... They were great value for money ... Three and a tanner for a seat on the stage ... where we were only eight feet from the pianist ... I'd found it a bit daunting the first time.'

'... As I recall it was a full orchestra'

'... so there was no sitting on the stage for you then ...'

'No ... we were standing to each side ... scanning the audience ... the only sitting we did was in a car parked across the street from where our target was staying.'

Jules believes he knows the answer to his next question, but he asks it all the same

'Do you remember what make the car was ...?

And his friend replies

'Yes ... even after all those intervening years ... It was a Riley Pathfinder ... '

Jules answers

' ... Thought it might have been ...'

and lets the conversation stop, but when the train makes its stop at 'Helensborough', he makes the excuse of needing some fresh air and stands at the open carriage door so he might search the platform for a glimpse of her, but she is not there. And when the train has gathered too much speed for anyone to jump off he returns to his seat.

He does the same at 'Dunbarton', but he knows this quest is hopeless and he returns to sit opposite his elderly friend who has, without the stimulus of conversation, fallen hard asleep. So, once settled back in his seat, he remove a page from his sketchbook to write a note – just in case he can pick her out from the inevitable crowd which will fill the platform at Queen Street Station – or the concourse – or the streets outside. She might even be in a queue waiting for a telephone to become free – or be in front of him when they reach the taxi rank.

Dear Wendy,

My Shhhh model of 'sixty three'

Thank you for your confidences,
Your words which broke my heart

I had so much to learn
And now, if I had known Holly was yours

(Could she be ours?)

I might have asked her to carry a first kiss from me to you

The first of all those many I yearned to place that day,
In vain hope they might heal your body and comfort you,

But for love of Sukie,
Or perhaps for want of courage,
I dared not.

Jules X

End Notes

Folio 3

1. Jules's eighty-one year old friend has a terminal illness and is relishing every day his life is spared

Folio 4

2. After meeting the American artist Richard Hamilton, 'The Hidden Persuaders' has become essential reading for those students who might wish for a career in the world of advertising.

Folio 7

3. Sukie's ring had a single perfect white pearl held in a silver mount formed like a lovers knot. It was *their* unofficial engagement ring, but also a symbol of Sukie's purity (her maidenhood) a fact her father would not know, even beyond his last gasp, or the damage he could have done by declared it worthless. It had been a cruel act and one Jules would never forgive.

Folio 11

4. Jules's father is being blinded by an inoperable tumour growing deep within his brain.

Folio 26

5. The words conveyed a sentiment which filled the school – 'Sukie when the sky above is full of clouds, or we are downcast for any reason, your presence makes the sun shine. So please don't ever change.'

Folio 26

6. Sukie wished this letter to be with Jules quickly so she entrusted it to a loyal and trusted friend who delivered it by hand to his parent's house the very next day. But Jules had already left for London and it was lost amid the confusion which was the prelude to, and then the aftermath of, his father's premature death. It will be three decades before Jules reads it.

Folio28

7 The three had imagined they might be swallowed-up by it and become entangled in a latter day Dickens novel, especially when they were invited down a side street to meet 'Our Nancy', an invitation the three had declined as graciously as they could; each in their turn protesting both lack of time and funds for such an indulgence.

Folio 28

8 The first time the young trio used the launderette they must have interrupted some sensational chatter, because they'd not been there more than a very few minutes – trying to get to grips with the huge and unfamiliar machines – when they were relieved of their task and ordered to return in an hour or so, but only after they had been relieved of the required coins.

Folio 32

9 An artist's model might work a full week at the Art School and earn just ten or twelve

pounds, while each of the girl dancers – in just that one evening – could 'make' a hundred.

Folio 34

10. The two young butchers are the only locals they know who 'let down' this otherwise 'Fab' community of shopkeepers.

Folio 38

11. It had turned out a rather gentle shade of blue-grey, which colour was ok when it was a bed cover, but not bright enough to work as a reflector and soften the contrast enough for Jules.

Folio 42

12. The advertisement featured Jean Shrimpton posed in a school-room dressed, like the many school-girls clustered around her, wearing a white blouse which is a little tight for her and a short box pleated skirt. The only difference is, while the girls are wearing strap-over school shoes and white ankle socks – Miss Shrimpton is wearing white calf length boots with heels.

Folio 53

13. After discovering their geography teacher (Miss Spill) had served on the committee to determine if it should be published in paperback, seven girls from Woodford County High had contributed sixpence each out of their pocket money towards the purchase of a copy of 'Lady Chatterley's Lover.'

The paperback was obtained the next day from the bookstand at London Bridge Station and quickly wrapped in brown paper and re-named, in bold letters, 'Latin for Today' and in this guise the girls had taken turns to read passages out-loud to the others at lunch times, sometimes under the noses of their teachers.

And in the stated spirit of the school '... to stimulate and feed the enquiring mind...' the daring Seven were now, after drawing straws, experimenting.

Folio 60

14 The two had no word, or words, to describe what they did together – for them they were sharing and enjoying a new and exciting experience – unique to them.

Folio 62

15. They could have walked there – lost in her heaven – for ever, but the Angel Sukie would eventually allow her eyes to close and the energy – which might have held his body hovering over her for an eternity – would fade and reveal him a mortal man whose arms quickly filled with pain and, for fear of crushing her, made him kneel beside her to gaze open her in wonder.

16. Jules's tiny room was always shaded from sunlight, but by some fluke, at that very moment, someone in a building nearby must have opened a window which reflected a beam

of sunlight – to be reflected and reflected again until it 'found' Sukie.

Folio 63

17. Jules is not an athlete and the muscles in his arms, shoulders and back should have screamed with pain and failed him in a fraction of the time they held him airborne over Sukie.

Folio 63

18. These narrow stairs had claimed the dignity of several students during that same semester, due to them having very high risers and very short treads.

Folio 64

19. An electrical component comprised of alternate layers of conducting and insulating materials, capable of storing electrical energy.

20 Jules's father was, in his youth, a keen experimenter and builder of electrical apparatus.

Folio 65

21 Charles Augustine Coulomb, who lived 1736 to 1806, was – if one was to judge him by his portrait – a serious, if not a sombre man who didn't often let his hair down – but faced with Sukie...

Folio 69

22. None of the College Photographic studios are finished or in use and all resemble untidy storerooms.

Folio 73

23. All had to be on a make-do and mend basis as the first instalments of their Scholarship grants were still unpaid.

Folio 79

24. The technician had asked the pair to wait nearby until they knew the negatives were good … 'in case they had to be re-taken'.

Folio 86

25. This beautiful natural place was, for Jules, a place of healing and forgiveness.

Folio 89

26. Sukie told Jules that a drink she'd been told was 'a Whisky and something' had tasted so awful it had made her feel ill. And the party had been a total flop too ... The best part, she said, was in the morning ... waking up very early and going exploring ... and finding some French windows ... and when she opened them ... discovering a garden ... a fab garden with a high wall around it ... a garden so secret, and so pretty, and so perfect, and so full of birdsong and the scent of roses that, almost before she knew it, she'd stepped out of her nightdress and was part of it ...

She'd stood still at first ... her slender limbs 'frozen' by the cool of the air ... but when she heard a Robin sing its invitation she ran ... spinning and dancing through and between the apple trees ... ducking under their heavy bows .... while following it's sweet song from this tree to that ... his charm enticing her ... inviting her into open spaces and past beds of roses heavy with intoxicating scent ...

All is leading her further and further away from the house ... until eventually it was out of sight and there was nothing around her but natural things ... a place where she could imagine herself as perfect as him ... a small bird ... his partner ... and as free as him in the morning air, or, when she looked down at herself to find a young woman – a Faerie, who would, on such a morning as this, bathe herself in pure sunlight and armfuls of sparkling dew. But when she did this she discovered her adventure must end because she believed her period had started.

27. Jules later realised that the happiness drug 'Librium' might have had some influence on his Angel's wonderful adventure in the garden.

Folio ~~122~~ 91

28. The 'Otis' passenger-lifts are very fast, so much so that at the request of the students' representatives, the fitters have been asked to return and make them softer in operation.

Folio 93

29. Jules is studying graphic design and photography, but has an ambition to be a film-maker and work in Television.

Folio 95

30. That afternoon, Jules and Sukie had talked of the feelings they had for each other. Feelings which they imagined might be love, but they

only knew for certain as an overwhelming desire to be fore-ever together and for time to stand still so they might remain together and naked.

And if there were serpents around they were impotent and devoid of influence – banished to live in and remain forever in the polluted corners in the minds of others. And when Sukie had stood in the doorway of his room as perfectly beautiful and charmingly androgynous as David in Donatello's amazing sculpture – Triumphant; Long haired; long limbed; small breasted – and with that wonderfully formed tummy – and Jules believed she'd made his room into a Heaven.

Folio 99

31. Jules's dream is of a fantastical future time with his Sukie created not by any contrivance or selfishness or even happenstance, but by the natural oneness they feel for each other.

Folio 105

32. The clothes are becoming more and more mixed up – like the images and ideas in Jules's head – and the naked girl is rummaging through them both.

Folio 109

33. She is performing this part of her dressing slowly – almost reluctantly – as if she is enveloping not just her Donatello tummy, but protecting something even more precious.

Folio 111

34. Roger's fried eggs and bacon must be, and will be perfect, with not a hint of a burnt edge anywhere.

Folio 112

35. The three students take turns to manage the housekeeping – This week it is Rogers turn.

Folio 115

36. Lez was always boasting that he could have sex with any girl or grown woman of his choosing and would, without exception, leave them 'exhausted, stuffed stupid, legless and begging for more.'

Folio 115

37. It had been an exciting afternoon – The petite Angelique driving him from the Art School to his flat in her mum's Triumph Herald – ostensibly so he could take a few 'strictly none glamour' photographs for her to enter a beauty competition and later some, for herself and her fiancée, of her looking 'Not so boring, glum looking, or prissy'.

And, after the kiss (it was her look, a tiny tear in her eye and the glossy lipstick that got the better of him) more of her with her high necked jumper discarded in favour of a shirt. And after a coffee-break, still more of her without that garment or her bra, so her pretty head, neck and bare shoulders might peep out from under the bedcover. Unforgettable!

Folio 115

38. A contact strip is a multiple print on a single piece of photographic paper. The resulting multi-print gives an overview of the poses and the comparative density of the negatives.

Folio 116

39. On hearing this Jules could not help but recall the man who'd looked so out of place at the college; the man with the wide shoulders and the suit which was far too expensive for him to be a tutor, and the stiff arm which had made Jules imagine a he may have a shoulder holster.

Folio 120

40. The Marquee is (in 1963)) a popular dance and Jazz venue, situated beneath the Academy Cinema in London's Oxford Street, where R and B (Rhythm and Blues) bands played on Thursday nights and Trad' Jazz on Saturdays. It had been previously The Academy Ballroom.

Everyone refers to it as a club, but no membership is required, or proof of age, as only soft drinks are sold on the premises – you just pay at the door and enjoy the music and dance.

Inevitably the obligatory crash doors (in case of fire) open onto a narrow cobbled back street with a convenient Pub. However a 'bouncer' – an OK guy – guards the girls who might be under eighteen as if they were his own.

Folio 124

41 There are both lever and Yale locks on the maisonette door, but the trio only ever use the Yale.

Folio 131

43 It feels to Jules as though a magnetic field is holding them both together and apart.

Folio 134

44. The area is undergoing extensive re-development and homeless people have formed a kind of 'collective' on the waste ground opposite the new College, where, when not scavenging for fuel, they sit huddled to windward of a huge fire – Jules has tried to photograph the scene from the college roof, but although the flames and sparks were spectacular, all his attempts had failed for want of a tripod or film speed, or both.

Folio 136

45. Jules imagined it might feel like this if in the heat of battle, when all things might seem to take place in extreme slow-motion, he was shot by a ball of .303 calibre ammunition – its size would be just right – and, he supposed, it would feel warm too.

He'd even waited for the pain to arrive, but it didn't – and when undressing for bed that night he'd looked to see if there was a mark – any evidence of her entering him – but there was none. But still he could feel she was there, snuggled down and safe inside him, a memory which over time would be lost to consciousness, to be awakened in a distant future by words overheard on a train.... and later still, with hard evidence when, after this story was written, this photograph of the girl he called 'Wendy' came to light ... an Angel's face ... but Shhhhhhhh, dear reader ... not a word ... We must let her sleep once more ... next his heart.

Printed in Poland
by Amazon Fulfillment
Poland Sp. z o.o., Wrocław